The Rewrapped Mummy

by Patrick MacAdoo

The Rewrapped Mummy

© 2015 Nightman Publishing

ISBN - 978-0-990-9656-4-0

Printed in the United States of America

Chapter One

Kirk pressed the toe of his boot's sole onto the mop's head. He used his foot to scrub the saturated mass over the coffee droplets dried onto a square of the marble floor. His scuffs caught the rhythm of the New Orleans Jazz blaring through his earbuds. He meant to work the brassy energy into his own stuff, maybe weave a few rays of sunshine into his otherwise gloomy, grungy, blues-rock. Lesley *loved* N'awlins Jazz.

He studied the speckled black marble for other spills. He'd already done an extra-special cleaning of the two public floors below. He could get away with a half-assed job up here, but he'd established a high standard for the administrative floor, and he intended to meet that standard. The math was simple: the longer he spent cleaning this floor, the better odds that he would bump into her.

He shrugged. He'd make up the lost time by blowing off the basement work. Nobody would notice. As usual, Lesley worked later than everybody else. He wouldn't be surprised if she fussed straight through the night over the final touches for the new exhibit, opening tomorrow. She wouldn't give a good goddamn about the basement.

He resumed his mopping, syncing the back and forth swishing to the brassy beat in his earbuds, but he focused on the rehearsal of the talking points aimed to impress Lesley. *The Rewrapped Mummy.* He chuckled. As far as he could tell, their humble museum had scored quite a coup. After its North American tour, extensive DNA testing promised to end the big mystery once and for all.

Grave robbers might have ripped the mummy from an Egyptian tomb, or perhaps from some anonymous potter's field. Either way, British con men passed the mummy off as one Pharaoh or another all throughout the Victorian era. Wealthy marks displayed the mummy in their parlors while the 'Egyptologists' extracted 'donations' for further excavations. Maybe the only thing Victorian aristocrats loved more than to host an exclusive exhibit was to expose a social rival's involvement in a fraud. The mummy eventually fell into the hands of an enterprising pair of swindlers, who played this hustle over and over again, one posing as the mummy's steward, and, after he'd milked the victim dry, the other, posing as an investigator, would, for a price, tip off the victim's fiercest (and richest) adversary. After they'd exhausted the scam in the U.K., they'd toured Continental Europe.

Kirk smirked. The swindlers' act came to a tragic end in Bulgaria, but not at the command of some outraged Slavic count. The murky details suggested a murder-suicide. The bloodshed, however, did no harm to the mummy's reputation. Sometimes bequeathed, sometimes sold, sometimes part of the spoils of one overthrow or another, the mummy remained a prized possession of the Balkan nobility right up to World War II. The mummy spent the war in Nazi hands, and after the fall of the Third Reich, the mummy vanished behind the Iron Curtain. Rumors placed the mummy in the Russian underworld up until the turn of the century, when an Oligarch gifted the artifact to a cousin holding a curatorship at a small British museum. Superficial testing revealed the mummy's elaborate sarcophagus was bogus. Further scrutiny falsified the mummy's outer wrapping. However, some of the layers proved authentic, albeit patched together from different sources. The layers led to the moniker, The Rewrapped Mummy, which stuck. The legitimate wrapping prompted a probe that uncovered the mummy's history and dead-ended at the British flimflam men. However, the mummy's adventures hadn't dead-ended. Curators discovered that the mummy had gone missing from storage, and years passed before it resurfaced through the efforts of a private collector, who struck a deal, in which the Rewrapped Mummy would complete a world tour, in order to recoup the collector's expenses, before returning to its home museum for extensive testing.

Kirk nodded. He had the bullet points down. He dunked the mop in the bucket. He wrung the head out as dry as he could. He would go into greater depth when she made follow-up chitchat. And somewhere in that chitchat he'd jump on the chance to steer the conversation to his band's upcoming gig.

A dryness crept up his throat. He coughed it away. He snorted. *Nerves.* Less than two weeks to whip the band into shape for their debut show. All the proven players in town knew all about his history. Wasted potential. One crash-and-burn project after another. He'd had to settle for a few young guys, who talked more than they walked, and partied more than they practiced. The situation had all the earmarks of a train wreck.

Out of the corner of his eye he caught rising motion on the stairwell. He took a deep breath to slow his heartbeat. He figured he must've been deep down inside himself or he would have seen Lesley leaving her office and going downstairs. She must've zipped out in order to escape his notice, but she sure was dragging ass up the steps.

His armpits went prickly and damp. If she actually agreed to go, the band could suck. He'd probably seem ridiculous, a twenty-nine year old dreamer fronting a band of kids. His hair would look thinner under a spotlight. Nobody might show up, just Lesley and few barflies.

He scoffed. Certain long-timers in the Portland scene, his 'frenemies,' cherishing grudges birthed back in his hotblooded days, had to be licking their lips, and whetting their knives, craving the next Kirk Taylor flameout. Of course each one of the assholes would bring their entourages. He set his jaw. He would face a hostile crowd, but a crowd nonetheless. If he didn't headbang too much, he might not reveal his quarter-sized bald spot, the sight of which would just *thrill* those assholes. He nibbled his lower lip. He still couldn't decide if a topknot would make his encroaching baldness obvious. He could wear it pulled back into a pony tail like at work, but Lesley had never seen him with his hair down, his best look.

He took a slow breath, which did nothing to calm his heartbeat. This move could backfire and ruin everything. If she said no, then things would turn awkward. He might even have to quit this cake job. If she said yes, she might end up feeling sorry for him, thinking he was an aging hipster who refused to grow up and get a life. Just a janitor dreaming of becoming a rock star.

He scrunched his eyes shut, then opened them wide. He'd almost psyched himself out. He couldn't go on like this, distracted, losing sleep. He had to roll the dice. He thumbed down the volume and took out his earbuds. A thud sounded from the stairwell. He frowned. Lesley's footsteps didn't sound like that.

Lesley squinted, but the fuzzy letters resisted her efforts to refocus them. She closed her eyes and leaned back as far as the office chair would go. She rubbed her eyelids. The bags beneath seemed to have sagged a million times heavier over the last two weeks' hectic workload. She calculated at least another hour and half of scanning documents, if she could get her fried brain to concentrate.

A low growl rumbled from deep in her guts and up through her throat. By dumb luck, she'd caught an error in Jeff's paperwork. Jeff hadn't worked a minute past 3 PM all week. Hell, he never had. Uncle Morty protected his lazy nephew's job. Cousin Jeff, the museum's office manager, dealt with the paperwork. He'd had two semesters of accounting, after all. He'd mixed up the cover pages for a bundle that Lesley needed to fill out and a bundle that needed to go to the donor. Scanning that page, Lesley had detected two errors before she realized the document didn't belong with her stuff. She'd given up trying to contact Jeff, who, tomorrow, would stroll in pretending he'd gone to bed and therefore didn't get her calls. She had to review all his work. If the donor thought for a second that they were trying to scam him out of even a fraction of his fee, he might exercise his opt-out clause and move the exhibit somewhere else. A facility like OMSI wouldn't feature the mummy, not like here, but the donor wouldn't have to worry about getting paid.

She massaged her temples against the simmering migraine. If the donor pulled out, the museum was done for. If the exhibit flopped, the museum was done for. Three decades of her family's work down the drain. The museum had been operating at a loss for years, as one relative or another indulged in vanity projects instead of overseeing profitable exhibits. As a result, the boutique museum's former stellar reputation had eroded to little more than a joke. But the family would blame her if the museum went belly-up on her watch.

She caught herself gnashing her teeth. She forced herself to relax. If the exhibit succeeded, the influx of cash would keep the doors open for a few more months. A successful exhibit would prove to potential donors that their collections could shine on the museum's center stage. Maybe, once the museum was back on its feet, she could stop working seventy-hour weeks. Maybe, once the curatorship of the museum had recaptured some of its former luster, she could hand the reins to one of her more capable cousins who was looking to beef up his or her resume. She could return to academia, teach Classics courses to eager grad-students who matriculated in that particular discipline for the pure love of it, because they were never going to earn a dime off of their doctorates. She smiled. She could go from the drudgery of scrutinizing legal documents to what she really loved to do, scrutinizing ancient texts. Of course, the same result held true if the museum went under …

The scorching heat of her blush withered her smile. She blinked her eyes until she got some moisture going. She leaned forward and stared at the document on top of the sheaf. She would just have to power through, that's all. She crinkled her forehead and delved into the first sentence, but the rhythmic swishes of Kirk's mop distracted her.

Her smile returned. She knew Kirk cherished a crush on her. Lean, scruffy, and intelligent, he had a certain amount of bohemian charm. But she didn't have time for such shenanigans. She imagined a casual roll would lead to a constant game of grabass here at work. She cringed. She couldn't deal with that. She sighed. The only other male attention she got came from the flirty old men who frequented the museum.

A muffled thud sounded from the stairwell outside her office. She frowned. Kirk's swishes came from the other end of the hall. She thought everybody else had gone home. Maybe she could rope whoever it was into giving her a hand with the paperwork.

She shoved her chair away from her desk. She groaned to her feet. Her thighs burned from the long day of climbing up and down the stairs. The service elevator was far too slow for her pace. At least she didn't have to worry about getting exercise. A whiff of spicy herb met her as she reached the doorway. Her eyes narrowed, then widened.

A hunched figure, wrapped head to toe … *no, not a costume.* The mummy lurched up another step. A joke, had to be a joke. *No joke.* She cranked her head towards Kirk, who mopped with his back to the stairwell. She opened her mouth, but couldn't make a sound, couldn't move another muscle.

Mid-pivot toward the stairs, Kirk halted. Lesley stood just inside the doorway of her office. A few stray strands had escaped from her ponytail. The black locks hung down to her eyebrows. The tasteful drape of her dark blue dress didn't disguise her curves.

Barefooted, having shucked her modest heels for the night … *damn*. He wanted to sweep her up in his arms and bearhug her.

He frowned. The whites of Lesley's eyes showed all the way around her irises. She gaped towards the stairwell. He resumed his pivot. His frown deepened into a scowl, then softened into a smirk. He scoffed. Somebody in a mummy costume took a shambling step up the stairs.

"Very funny," Kirk said. "Is this supposed to scare me?"

The guy in the mummy costume took another painstaking step up the stairs. Kirk's smile broadened. That Lesley would try so hard to play a joke on him, that could only mean that she liked him. His smile dimmed a notch. He warned himself, for the zillionth time, not to get carried away, like he always used to. If he was being honest with himself, they hadn't reached a level where she might pull this kind of stunt. At least he wouldn't have thought so.

He cocked his head toward Lesley. "Okay," he said. "Very …" Lesley didn't react. She appeared to not have moved at all. The mummy thumped up another step. Kirk caught a spicy whiff in the air. The mummy-guy's heavy thud sent vibrations through the marble that Kirk felt in his soles.

Kirk peered at the dude, who'd finally made it to the landing. A faint yellow stained the creases of the mummy-guy's bandages. The wrapping looked a thousand years old. The dude took a creaky step towards Lesley, who continued to gape at 'the mummy.' Kirk had to admire her dedication to the prank. She just kept selling absolute terror.

Kirk sniffed. He detected a sour hint under the gathering cloud of herbal spice. The mummy took another ridiculous lurch towards Lesley. Kirk shook his head. The dude's performance sucked, worse than the worst of schlocky monster-movies. Lesley let out a low, continuous wine. Kirk said, "Enough."

The mummy cranked its right arm towards Lesley. The arm's excruciating rise exposed a brownish tinge to its underside. The bandages encased the mummy's fingers mitten-style. The loose thumb twitched. Kirk narrowed his eyes. The bandages, so thick they almost smoothed the mummy's features, formed an unbroken wrap around the mummy's face. No eyeholes, no nose holes, no mouth hole, no way to breath.

Lesley's voice broke as she whispered, "Kirk."

The mummy's hand neared her face. Kirk charged the mummy. He speared the point of the mop's handle into the center of the mummy's chest. The impact jarred the mop out of Kirk's hand and rattled Kirk all the way up to his shoulder joints. The collision drove the mummy a step backwards.

Kirk grabbed Lesley's hand. He pulled her away from the mummy's sluggish lunge. Lesley's body stiffened. She sagged and collapsed against Kirk, who hustled her to the far side of the stairwell. She listed forward. He caught her before she toppled down the stairs. He drew her back, cinched his right arm around her waist, and helped her down the stairwell. He looked over his shoulder. The mummy took one lumbering step down the stairs.

Kirk's heel slipped off the edge of a riser and slammed into the next tread. His stumble threw them off balance. He scrambled to get his feet underneath himself. His boots slapped a manic beat down to next the landing. He skidded and jerked them to a halt.

Rigidity paralyzed Lesley's body. Her seizure strained against his grip. Her eyes rolled up into the back of her head. The mummy doddered over the handrail and pressed his shoulder against the wall as he descended another step into the stairwell's dimness. Kirk laid Lesley on the landing's cold marble and crouched beside her. All her muscles seemed to maintain contraction. He looked at the whites of her up-rolled eyes. No way was she faking it. The mummy trudged down another step.

Kirk's voice cracked as he yelled, "Enough! Call 911!"

An agonizing moment preceded the mummy's next blunt footfall. Kirk gave Lesley's cheek a series of light taps. He found her rapid pulse on her neck. He leaned his ear to her lips and felt her shallow breaths. He didn't know what to do. He twisted in his crouch toward the mummy, who clumped deeper into the stairwell's after-hours darkness. This couldn't be happening. Unless some psycho had spent hours wrapping himself, obsessing over the costume until it looked authentic, and planning his spree. Kirk nodded. That made sense.

He gathered Lesley in his arms. Her ramrod posture would not bend. He managed to squat-thrust to a standing position. Even her neck remained stiff. He pivoted on the landing and looked down the stairwell. He couldn't help imagining the two of them toppling down, his back broken, lying there while the mummy took his sweet time catching up to them.

He hurried into the second floor's main room. Lesley's stiff body jounced in his arms. With each stride into the darkened hall the backlash of Lesley's arched spine grew more violent. He slowed to a fast walk. As he passed exhibits, he kept one eye out for potential weapons. He couldn't remember if he closed the service elevator, he was supposed to after every use, because the elevator wouldn't move if the bay doors weren't shut. But sometimes he blew it off. If he did this time, they'd be trapped. Probably the mummy-guy had a knife, at the least. If the psycho had a gun, then they were fucked.

His arms slipped a few inches. He hoisted Lesley. He felt the gathering burn in his forearms and biceps. He remembered to breath. He reached the elevator bay. He thumbed the Call button. The elevator thunked as it engaged. He lowered Lesley to the marble floor and exhaled. He squinted into the shadowy main room. The psycho swayed into the entrance. The gloom made his costume and shuffling gait appear all the more authentic

The elevator's antique gears grated behind Kirk. He turned his back on the mummy's approach. He gripped the cast-iron handle and foisted the top hatch upward. The heavy metal barrier raked on its casters up into its housing within the upper wall. The top hatch's action engaged the lower hatch, which slid down into its housing.

The bottom of the elevator car shunted into the cobwebby shaft. A spicy scent overcame the shaft's mustiness. Kirk wheeled towards the main room. The mummy heaved his shoulder, his dead arm flopping, into his next torturous step, which carried him over halfway into the murky hall. The psycho's dementia had to be stupid-big to keep up this parody of a movie monster. Kirk massaged his own smarting shoulder. He wouldn't let the brittle-boned walk fool him. When he rammed the mop into the fucker, those bandaged muscles proved to be gym-rat solid. The hall's deep shadows gave the bandages around the mummy's face an ashy tint that further smoothed his features. Kirk scowled. *Impossible*. That thick, unbroken wrap … Kirk couldn't see how the psycho could breath.

He tore himself away from the weird sight. Lesley's rigid catatonia persisted. The dry wooden slats of the car's safety gate came into view. Kirk groaned into a dead lift of Lesley's inflexible frame. He shifted her from one awkward position to another. No way could he lift the gate with her in his arms. He laid her on the marble floor.

A closer thump reverberated in the hall behind him. He choked down the urge to look. He visualized what he had to do. The elevator had to come to a complete stop before the gate's lock would disengage. It would be faster to roll Lesley into the elevator. The image of pushing Lesley's body onto the dusty elevator made his guts clench.

Another thump brought a surge in the spicy cloud. A mini-headrush gouted static through Kirk's thoughts. He rocked back on his heels. He flailed his arms. He regained his balance. He whispered, "Whoa." Some kind of airborne drug. He nodded. That explained everything. The psycho reeked of the drug, which had to be the source of his delusion. If it came down to it, Kirk figured he should be able to kick the burnout's ass. That, or the drug would make the psycho superhuman, almost impossible to put down. Kirk's own experiences gave him a measure of immunity. And Lesley's lack of tolerance resulted in an overdose. He had to get her to a hospital. Some drug like this, something so new he'd never heard of it, had to be devastating.

The elevator car *shunked* into place. He seized the slivery slats. He heaved the gate open. He scooped up Lesley and lowered her to the dusty wooden floor. He slammed the gate down. He punched the first floor button. The elevator hitched as the upper and lower hatches shuttled toward one another.

The mummy's bandaged fist bashed in between a pair of the wooden slats, the blow shattering the wood. Splinters flew into Kirk's face and neck. Kirk flinched backward and tripped over Lesley. His ass hammered the floor. His back whammed into the car's back wall. The impact knocked the wind out of him. The hatch doors clamped shut.

Kirk sucked in a shuddery breath. The herbal fumes made him sneeze. Sandstorms raged over sun-baked dunes. He opened his eyes. He raised his calves off of Lesley's stomach. He levered himself up to his feet. Lesley remained motionless, as stiff as a board, her eyes wide open, with only a hint of her irises edging out from under her upper eyelids. One of the broken slats still hung together by a few fibers and swung an erratic pattern as the elevator clanked down the shaft.

Kirk drew a steadier breath. The spicy scent had dissipated, the customary musty odor reasserting itself. His head cleared. He knelt next to Lesley. He propped her upper back on his lap and cradled her head. He checked her pulse, which had slowed to a trance tempo. *Good.* Unless the psycho dropped the mummy delusion, they would get to the front door way before the weirdo could get down the stairs. He yanked the key ring out of the back pocket of his jeans and readied the front-door key. Once he got them outside, he'd yell his head off for help.

All four buttons on the elevator's control panel lit up. They winked out. The third floor button lit up and winked out. The second floor did the same thing faster. The first even faster, and the basement fastest. The light riffled through the floors, up and down, up and down, faster and faster, until they all lit up simultaneously. The top three lights died. The basement light glowed. Kirk swallowed. His dry as dust throat resisted the swallow, distorted it into a painful gag. *A trick.* The psycho must've fiddled with the settings. He nodded. Screwing with the elevator, no chance his victims would escape that way, that explained the psycho's total commitment to the mummy shtick.

Lesley gurgled. He forced her mouth open and made sure her tongue didn't obstruct her airway. He released her jaw. Her lips relaxed to a straight line, except for a slight droop at their right corner. He winced. Could be a stroke. Could be a permanent condition, or do permanent damage to her. Brain damage would destroy her, maybe make her suicidal.

He brushed the stray dark bangs off her smooth white forehead. He detected a slight jitter to the visible rims of her brown irises. *Like she was fighting it.* He hissed through gritted teeth, "C'mon girl."

The elevator banged against the shaft's bottom. The car shook to a stop. The hatch rumbled open. Kirk squirmed out from underneath Lesley. He rested her head on the elevator's dusty floor. He pawed the wall, bracing himself to his feet. He wobbled toward the busted gate. He inhaled. A dash of herb spiced the stuffy air.

The single low-wattage bulb outlined the jumble of crates and boxes. Narrow corridors between the ceiling-high stacks created a maze. The psycho could be creeping anywhere. Kirk took another breath. All around the basement's black fringes, hot blinding light forced him to shield his eyes. A new scent, sunlight scorching sand, reached his nostrils. The faint clink of chains, the faint cracks of whips, startled him. He blinked, and the all of these impressions evaporated.

A thump came from the other side of the room, halfway up the stairs. A louder thump followed. Kirk punched the third floor button, but it remained dark. He tried all the buttons. None worked. He lifted the busted gate. He tried to pull the hatch doors shut, but they wouldn't budge. He panted. He breathed in the spice. He swooned against edge of the bay. *Gas*. Like at the dentist. Obviously the psycho had some kind of oxygen mask on underneath the bandages, that's how he breathed. Snatches of the worst tortures from serial-killer TV shows flickered through Kirk's imagination. All of them involved straps and restraints, trays of medical instruments, and cold steel operating tables. A growing flare blotted these images from his mind. The noonday sun seared his naked back. Bluish afterimages doubled the other slaves, the whip-cracking masters, the massive base that was only half-built, the structure promising to drink the sweat and blood of lifetimes before completion. A profound thirst shriveled his throat. His hacking cough dispelled the mirage.

Kirk rubbed his face with his hands. *Can't be real*. He shoved himself upright. There was a door on the other side of the room. Connected to the basement of the church next door. Another thump sounded from the stairwell, near the basement landing. He studied Lesley. He doubted he could carry her to the door before the mummy reached the basement and blocked the way. But he could make it, if he ran *right now*.

His face blazed. He scanned the nearby crates. He spotted a crowbar. He staggered over and snatched it up. He retreated to the elevator's entrance. He looked over his shoulder. Lesley laid in the same place, unmoving. He turned his attention towards the far end of the narrow corridor.

Sluggish movement, implying contours, disturbed the murk. Kirk's front foot slid back a couple of inches. He squeezed the crowbar's handle. The metal felt thick and lethal. He willed his foot back to its original position.

A gritty scuff, grazing along the dusty concrete for what seemed like ages, raised Kirk's hackles, and ferried the mummy, no, *the psycho*, to the brink of the bulb's cone of hazy light, which yellowed the winding of the mummy's head and torso. Another scraping, tormented stride brought the mummy all the way into view. Shadows pooled in the mummy's shallow eye sockets and transformed the mummy's mouth into a grim, horizontal slash. The furrows marking the winding of the bandages seemed to deepen, the thick bandages seemed to swell. Kirk saw no bulge indicating an oxygen mask or tank. The parch in his throat reasserted itself and forced him to hack. He shook his head.

The mummy's bandaged sole scratched over the concrete, carrying the freak further into the feeble light. A slump burdened the mummy's arms, which remained as immobile as icicles despite the mummy's shambling pace. The hands … Kirk stared at the hands, the wrap encasing the four fingers, the thumbs jutting out. The wrapping wound unbroken all the way down the arms to the mummy's fingers. No way could the psycho do that by himself. Kirk tried to picture some kind of elaborate apparatus, spooling out the bandages while the psycho whirled in place, self-wrapping, but he couldn't bring such a machine into focus. *An accomplice.* He surged toward that explanation, kicking away from the madness thrashing all around him.

A blast of spice enveloped Kirk. He tried to snort the cloying scent out of his nostrils. He tried to hock it up out of his mouth. He coughed. His thirst regained his attention. Felt like grains of sand speckled his throat. His hollow belly rumbled, far beneath that thirst, which unfolded a sense of confinement. Rough wood pressing into his backside, crowding his elbows, a hair away from his nose. From outside, a flurry of pounding, fists and bare heels against planks. Best to lie still. Even if they managed to break free of their boxes, they'd never escape the sealed mausoleum. They'd die around the stone sarcophagus. Rumors slithered around the slums, whispering of other eternal servants, trapped, murdering each other, eating the flesh and drinking the blood of the slain. He feared he couldn't maintain the serenity necessary for a peaceful drift into endless servitude.

The clatter of the crowbar against the concrete floor jolted Kirk back to the basement. The mummy had advanced to the near side of the light bulb, the feeble glow limning the form of the mummy's body, a black void blotting out its foreparts. The mummy's left arm swung a few degrees with its next crooked stride. Between the mummy's right side and the stacks of boxes, a man-sized gap beckoned. Kirk twitched. He grabbed the crowbar

Kirk waggled his weapon. *Fuck this.* He charged. He brandished the crowbar in preparation to bash the mummy's brains out. He inhaled a dense hit of spice. A slight pressure against his knee mounted as he pistoned toward the mummy. On the descension of his leg, his heel seemed to plunge into an invisible slough of thickening mud. An icy cramp spread from his guts to his bowels as he first anticipated, then craved, and finally prayed to any gods that might be listening, that his foot would touch down on the concrete.

Relief washed over him when his sole slapped the concrete. Had to be the weird gas messing with his perceptions. He cocked the crowbar, letting the hooked end drop behind his shoulder. He was gonna crack the mummy's skull. He twisted his hips for a little extra torque, then he uncoiled, exploding towards the mummy. His reclaimed velocity fizzled. That muddy feeling, that underwater feeling, reasserted itself. His swing of the crowbar decelerated as the mummy raised a warding arm. The lift of mummy's defense caught up to Kirk's slowing attack, then overtook his braking arm.

Kirk growled through gritted teeth, channeling more force into his swing until his arm trembled and sweat dappled his forehead, but the deceleration continued, and his growl climbed to a scream as the mummy's hand clamped onto his wrist.

An electric bolt rocketed through Kirk's central nervous system. His spine arched backward until his bones crackled. His eyes rolled up into his head, but he saw, he *felt* … music … in the firing of a synapse he understood everything that had baffled him, that had eluded him, before … he not only perceived all his mistakes, his missed opportunities, but also realized the corrections that would make his every song a hit, no, *a masterpiece*. And then all of it vanished, leaving a withering vacuum behind. But something remained, something that had nothing to do with music.

Lesley noticed herself as an entity separate from the bright warmth. The over-spilling sensation slowed. She ceased her vain struggle to capture it *all*. She relaxed into the manageable stream until she detected a draining effect, and she surged into the attempt to salvage as much as she could before all was lost. The brightness dimmed, the warmth chilled. She flew backwards. Darkness surrounded the brightness, which shrank from a supernova to a pinprick. The cold damp, threatening to reinstate her erstwhile benightedness, sank into her skin. Her every cell cried out to return to the light, which winked out into total darkness. A suicidal void welled up inside her. For a moment, or an aeon, she couldn't tell, she wallowed, then she beat the void back. She *would* find a way back. She had to.

She smelled spice. She opened her eyes. The gloom reminded her of the family business, the failing museum, her responsibility, the unfairness, how hard she worked … she let out a low moan. The dark ceiling, the metal walls, too close, far too close. Cold hardness jabbed all along her backside.

Her tight neck muscles forced a groan out of her as she raised her head. The shattered wooden gate made her frown. She located herself in the elevator … she remembered the stairwell, the top floor, but everything between then and now yawned blank. She splayed her arms to press herself up to a sitting position, and her deltoids, biceps, triceps, and forearms burned. She bit back a yip. Tears blurred her vision. She ground through the pain and levered her torso upright. All her muscles seemed to throb, even her abs.

She raked her forearm across her eyes. The hazy yellow light meant she'd descended to the basement. She mouthed, "How?" *They are coming … we must escape*! The warning and the imperative echoed inside her skull. The identity of *they* eluded her. *We* did not.

Her eyes found Kirk. Long clumps of his long brown hair had worked free of his ponytail. Kirk held a crowbar high over his head, as if to brain the mummy, who gripped Kirk by that wrist, arresting Kirk's attack. She quailed. Kirk could damage, perhaps even destroy the mummy, destroy the *miracle*.

She opened her mouth wide and put all the breath in her lungs into the effort, but only a feeble squawk came out. She gulped more air. She screamed, "No!"

The crowbar fell from Kirk's grasp, flipping end over end. Its hooked end banged against the concrete and ricocheted into the air, propelling its bladed end which slapped against the floor and shot upward, levering the hooked end back against the concrete. As the arc of crowbar's seesawing collisions diminished, the clattering accelerated, the maddening crescendo terminating in a clank that startled Lesley out of her daze.

The basement's yellowish gloom hindered her inspection, but the integrity of the mummy's winding seemed undisturbed. Her exhalation stretched into a relieved sigh.

Her spine whip-cracked into straightness. There was no time for rest. Kirk's play at heroics had only wasted time, which was sifting downward to the last grains of sand. The mummy meant them no harm. The mummy promised an untold wealth of knowledge, which would be lost to them, forever, if they didn't get a move on, *immediately*.

She scrunched her eyes shut but she couldn't penetrate her inner fog, she couldn't pinpoint the exact nature of the threat, just like she couldn't recollect the fields of the mummy's knowledge, but she knew the peril loomed and would rob the earth-shattering wisdom from her forever. The fact that the mummy, whether a two-centuries old hoax or not, had reanimated, proved to her that she'd lucked into the presence of a miracle that required every and any sacrifice to preserve.

She opened her eyes. The mummy released Kirk's wrist. The mummy's head wilted, his chest sagged, but he stayed on his feet. Kirk staggered backwards. He tripped and slammed onto his butt. The knuckles of his right hand hinged on the concrete, inches away from the crowbar.

She thrust herself to her feet. The sudden motion caused her sprung hamstrings to cramp. She cried out and flopped to all fours. The cramps relaxed enough to allow her to crawl towards Kirk. She had to explain to him that the mummy needed them. She palmed Kirk's shoulder.

Kirk craned his head towards her. His green eyes bulged, his nostrils flared. "We gotta get him outta here …" He swallowed, and he lowered his voice while saying, "They're coming. A cult. If they get him …" His brow furrowed. She thought confusion muddled his attempt to make her understand. He said, "I can't explain it."

"Help me up."

They managed to prop each other up. Kirk stationed himself between her and the mummy. He regarded the mummy. He bent his knees. He raised his hands in front of his chest. He seemed more intent on saving her than the mummy. He still didn't comprehend.

From the ceiling on the other end of the basement, where the rains had damaged the flooring of the first-floor delivery entrance, a hushed creak upset the silence. Soft but quick footfalls pattered overhead across the marble aisle. She imagined a black-clad paramilitary team. She shivered. They intended to steal the mummy away from the museum, away from the world, away from *her*.

Kirk whispered, "They'll search the main floors first. We gotta get moving." His stride grew more sure as he approached the mummy and slung one of the mummy's arms over his shoulder.

She hurried as fast as her tight legs would go. She laid the mummy's heavy arm across her shoulders. The rough bandages abraded her skin through her dress's material. A strong blast of mustiness made her avert her nose. She strained under the mummy's colossal weight. The mummy felt as immobile as one of the museum's stanchions. The corner of her mouth twitched. Perhaps the reanimation had burned the mummy out, had depleted whatever power he had left. Perhaps, the stress had made her snap, a stroke, maybe, and all this was just a delusion.

The grinding of hip bone on pelvic socket traveled through the mummy's frame and vibrated into Lesley's body, as he took an agonizing step. The vibrations transformed into an electric surge, which carried her close to that bright warmth. She sensed the proximity of stupendous knowledge. The wave of energy receded, but left her tingling, and she felt Kirk's intentions. The connecting door to the church basement. She knew the alarm code for the sensor, but tripping the alarm could buy them some time if the security company reacted fast enough to slow their adversaries. The mummy continued to act as a conduit between them. The museum was no longer important. She quashed the twinge of guilt with the truth that the mummy's gifts could change the world. They had to save the mummy, whatever the cost. Kirk agreed, wholeheartedly.

Kirk grasped the doorknob with his free hand. He watched the black box affixed at shoulder-height on the adjacent wall. The box's red light started to flash when he opened the door. Leslie's relief flowed through the mummy to him, and buoyed him, as they shared the hope that the security company would respond quickly enough to foil the cult from capturing him.

Lesley faltered. Kirk shifted deeper under the mummy and took on more of the stunning burden as the three of them passed over the threshold. Low-wattage florescent tubes lit the church's boiler room. On the left, rows of folded metal chairs leaned against the wall. Haphazard stacks of cardboard boxes cluttered the path to the stairwell. The church's enormous furnace dominated the right wall. Silver, accordion-ribbed ducts tentacled from the rectangular body of the furnace and coiled across the ceiling. Cobwebs draped from every nook and cranny. Dust gritted under their soles. The sandpapery rhythm ignited his synapses, in his mind's ear he heard an entire song, no, an entire project's worth of songs, in less than a blink of his eye, each measure, each beat, perfect and true. He basked in the afterglow of both creation and the auditory experience, as he replayed the music again and again. He filed the work of art away. Lesley's burning desire to save the mummy flowed over the fading music. *Sorry.* He had to focus. She had felt his attention slipping away. From the mummy, he absorbed the danger, that the cult, in fact, *cults*, wanted the mummy for themselves, to probe the mummy's secrets for their own shadowy purposes. Otherwise, the mummy's inner world, to Kirk, was as cold, dark, and empty as a moonless desert midnight. Lesley, on the other hand, seemed wide open, so he had to assume that she was privy to his heart of hearts too. He'd already transmitted their best shot. She knew the password to get her into his buddy's militia compound, which was more or less a place for those rednecks to shoot their guns and dry their weed crop. Lesley and the mummy would be safe there, they could rest and regroup, figure out their next move, figure out if they could trust the authorities. She'd take his car, she knew his spare key was on the magnet in the left rear wheel-well of his Subaru.

At the far end of the room a rickety wooden stairwell led up into the darkness. Kirk steeled himself. With an audible popping of his spine, the mummy stepped away from Kirk's support. An immediate draining sensation shriveled Kirk's bliss. He filled his lungs with the spicy fumes. His consciousness soared, then drifted downward.

Kirk slumped. He yearned to return to that state of musical grace. It wasn't all gone, but the easy genius of it had evaporated. The urge to reach out, to reestablish contact, amplified to within an eyelash of irresistible. Jealousy, towards Lesley's continued bond with the mummy, spiked through his heart. She must still be experiencing her fondest wish. A double shot of guilt washed away his envy. He ached to reconnect to her through the mummy. He bowed his head. During their linkage, he'd received no feedback from her, only her overwhelming resolve to save the mummy. He raised his head and gazed at her as she helped the mummy towards the stairs. That was it. Her resolve grew so huge that it eclipsed whatever else her heart contained. He hoped his own obsession hadn't blocked that he was doing this for her as much as for what the mummy promised him.

The mummy's steps seemed more sure, he seemed to lean less on Lesley. Kirk couldn't help a little smile at her tenacity. Barefoot, her dark blue dress hampering her range of movement, the black topknot of her ponytail rising maybe an inch above the mummy's shoulder, she was *not* about to give up. The mummy stood straighter, his stride grew longer and faster as they neared the stairwell.

A pang wrung Kirk's guts. He might never see them again. That musical insight, which pierced that slimy veil that he always knew, goddamn it, he *knew* it had always been there, weighing him down, crushing him, that penetrating virtuosity had already burned off to mere wisps. He intuited that a longer merging with the mummy would make the insight not only deeper but also permanent. He would be a god of any genre he undertook.

At the foot of the stairwell, Lesley turned her head and locked eyes with Kirk. His breath caught in his throat. Somebody had to slow down their adversaries. Her steady gaze bolstered him. He managed to nod. Once they reunited, he'd tell her everything. She and the mummy started up the stairs. Kirk took one last look at her. He forced himself to face the door to the museum.

His vision went fuzzy. He listened to their tread on the steps. Just a few moments ago their soft rhythm would have inspired a magnum opus. Nothing came to him. The door at the top of the stairs wheezed open. Their footsteps above faded to silence. He thought he heard a boot heel *thock* against concrete on the other side of the museum's door. He stole over to the metal folding chairs. He took one and brought it back to the door. He wedged the upper edge of the chair's back under the doorknob. He tested the tension of the makeshift jam. The chair vibrated. *Too much give.*

He chewed his lower lip. No lock secured the door. The church and the museum operated on the honor system. He narrowed his eyes. Maybe they wouldn't know … but the attempted wedge would give him away. He swept the chair away from the door. He'd carried it halfway back to the stacks when the door opened.

He expected black-clad paramilitary types, not the drab windbreakers and jeans of the crew that clambered through the doorway. Some wore ball-caps. Most of the half-dozen seemed as old as his dad. But they all pointed shiny black handguns at him.

A bald white man advanced toward Kirk. The man's jacket didn't disguise his brick-house build. He said, "Where is it?"

Kirk stared into the man's bloodshot eyes. He eased the chair down to the floor. He raised both hands over his head. He made his eyes bug.

"I know you're the museum's janitor," the bald man said. "Kirk Taylor, age twenty-nine, failed musician. Now, tell me where it is."

Kirk struggled to keep the anger off his face.

"We don't care about you," the bald man said. "Do you understand me? We could let you go and never bother you again." The bald man's eyebrows dipped into a deep V. "Or, we could kill you."

Kirk gaped at the bald man. He tried to look as dumb as possible. He let his jaw go a little slack. So they knew who he was. They probably knew that somebody tripped the alarm. So he couldn't pretend that cleaning the church was part of his job. An idea made his scalp tingle. He said. "Okay. I'm not gonna die over this."

Some of the gunmen relaxed a little. The bald man did not.

Kirk pitched his voice near falsetto range while blurting, "Miss Bosh paid me twenty bucks to set off the alarm and come in here and make noise! She didn't tell me why and she sure as shit didn't say nothing about no men with guns!"

He strove to strike a chord of innocence in the heat of the bald man's glare. If this worked, he could catch up to them in no time at all. If it didn't … he didn't know how long he could hold out if they tortured him.

The bald man said, "Take him."

Chapter Two

Lesley glanced at the gas gauge. The white needle vibrated right next to the red E slash. Nothing but green stretched in front of her. The weeds grew waist-high. Moss coated the massive trunks of trees. The dense canopy stained the sunlight green. Wherever a stray shaft managed to penetrate the lush green leafage, green spores swarmed in the balmy yellow ray.

The Subaru shuddered. Lesley jerked the steering wheel. She peered into the verdant latticework and guided the Subaru back onto the dirt ruts. Pliable branches scratched along the Subaru's sides before whipping back into place. The shuddering continued. She eased her bare foot off of the gritty gas pedal until the ride smoothed out. A runnel of sweat trickled from her forehead and stung into her eye. She wiped her forehead, the motion straining the material of her blue dress, which clung to her damp skin.

She checked the rearview mirror, which she'd angled to reflect the backseat. The grungy old orange and brown afghan covered the mummy. If she stared, she could make out the mummy's sallow bandages through the crocheted loops of yarn. She wondered if the mummy was burning up under the blanket. She wondered if the mummy felt anything at all. He hadn't moved a muscle since they left Portland. She inhaled. The cumin and clove scent lingered, but a smidgen of rot caused her preoccupied sniffs. She couldn't pinpoint the source, whether the odor emanated from the mummy or Kirk's dirty car.

She shook off the distraction. She refocused on the almost imperceptible 'road' ahead. The impressions she'd gleaned from Kirk still shone strong. But maybe he'd remembered wrong. Maybe she'd taken a wrong turn. She was all but certain that everything looked the same out here in the sticks. If she hit some dead end, she didn't know if she could drive the Subaru in reverse along this trail. She chewed the tip of her tongue. Wouldn't matter anyways. They would run out of gas. Hikers got lost and died in the Oregon wilderness all the time. She'd never hiked, never camped in her life.

She caught a glint of metal in the green. She squeezed the steering wheel. The aluminum gate appeared between the boles of two humongous redwoods, just like in the images Kirk had transmitted to her. She exhaled. She took her foot off the gas. The rutted lane sapped the Subaru's pace. Armed men emerged from the thickets. She stomped the brake pedal. She rocked with the car's sudden stop.

Their head-to-toe camouflage blended with the woods and confused their numbers. She zeroed in on their gleaming black assault rifles and counted five sentries. Two took up positions in front of the gate. The others stalked around the car, their legs swishing through the thigh-high brush. She tried to keep her head still while tracking their inspection. One of them stopped by the rear passenger window on her side. He must be scrutinizing the shape under the blanket in the back seat. He couldn't think anything else but 'dead body.' He probably wouldn't act so brazen if Kirk was here. She winced. She'd had no choice. The mummy came first.

A headrush overwhelmed Lesley. She lowered her chin to her chest and closed her eyes. She exhaled. *A bad one*. Not the worst. A couple of times, she'd had to pull over to the shoulder of the road and wait for the spell to pass. She couldn't tell if the mummy's radiation caused the dizziness, or if she'd simply had a stroke and the fits were the consequences of her diseased brain attempting to resurface to reality.

"Who the fuck are you?"

Lesley flinched. She'd spaced out for so long that she'd forgotten to prepare for this part. She swallowed the lump in her throat. Her questioner loomed above her open window. The bill of his camouflage cap shadowed all but the hard planes of his cheeks and jaw. Around the barrel of his black assault rifle, his grip whitened his bony knuckles. Lesley cleared her throat and said, "Krakatoa."

He stared at her. He sucked his teeth. "You look government to me. Why don't you turn the fuck around and get the fuck out of here."

Gizmo. The name surfaced out of the data Kirk had transmitted to her. *Asshole* bobbed up right behind the tall, thin guy's name. A wave of exhaustion pulled her away from dredging up more information. She couldn't help trying to calculate the last time she had slept and the last time she had ate. She couldn't force her way inside the compound. Even if she managed to walk back to civilization, this imbroglio would ruin her. Forget about academia. She wouldn't be able to land a job at anything close to matching her qualifications. That was, if she didn't end up in an institution, just another Bosh family whackjob. She gnashed her teeth. She probably didn't have to worry about that stuff. Chances were, the cult was hot on her heels. If they didn't let her in, then she was dead meat.

An involuntary tremor vibrated through her skull. "Jake," she said. "Call Jake."

Gizmo clucked his tongue. He leaned away from the window and the shadows left his face. His beady eyes swept over his comrades.

"Gizmo," Lesley said.

The sound of his name made him twitch. His eyes returned to her.

"Tell Jake that Kirk sent me," Lesley said.

Gizmo snapped his mouth shut. Lesley shifted her gaze to the gate. She heard one of the others mutter into a walkie-talkie. She kept the smile off her lips, but she could've sworn she felt Gizmo's confusion rise near to panic. Prison, yes prison, might've taught him to hide his fear under a hardass demeanor, but she had rocked him back on his heels, no doubt about it. But rubbing it in, she sensed, could be very dangerous.

One of the others approached Gizmo. He turned his back to Lesley, but she heard him rasp, "Jake says let her in."

She exhaled. Her shoulders dropped into a more relaxed posture. A burly man, wearing the same fatigues as the others, swung the gate open. She depressed the gas pedal just enough to get the Subaru rolling. The weeds massed even higher on the other side of the gate. She glanced in the rearview. The squad of men secured the gate and prowled behind the Subaru. Gizmo's thin lips moved. The burly guy bobbed his square head. Lesley harbored no doubts about their discussion. She supposed the best thing was to let them think she had a dead body in the back seat. If they found out anything close to the truth, they might decide to take the mummy for themselves.

She piloted the car around an S-curve and into the compound. A pack of pitbulls charged at the Subaru. Lesley braked. The dogs, yapping, blasted through the tall grass, running rings around the car. A sharp whistle called them back to the men striding towards her. Four of the men wore tee-shirts and khaki shorts. The fatigues of the rest matched the uniforms of the squad behind her. They all carried guns. Including those trailing her, she estimated their numbers at fifteen. The gnarled trees walling in the compound, the moss-splotched cabin, and the neat configuration of six super-sized pickups parked next to a shack, provided excellent cover for snipers.

Her eyelids seemed to weigh a ton. *This was a mistake.* She crinkled her eyes shut and then opened them, but her eyeballs remained dry as dust. *Stuck.* These men could take the mummy, they could do anything they wanted. She looked beyond their compound. A field of lush weeds stretched towards a distant treeline. She could gun it. The Subaru was narrow. She might luck out and find a way through forest. They might decide she wasn't worth chasing. She detected flecks of white in the remote green. She stared at them until they became obvious. Targets. The silhouette kind, she guessed, like at shooting ranges, the scores higher at the lethal locations. Shooting up the Subaru wouldn't even challenge their skills. They'd probably let her get halfway across the field just to make it interesting.

Wisps of smoke brought her attention back to the compound proper. She'd missed the semicircular brickwork on the first glance. A barbecue pit. She'd interrupted their cookout. She let out a silent scoff. Her encounter with the cult had made her jump to conclusions, had made her fear that something sinister lurked beyond every corner. These guys were just a bunch of good ol' boys who liked to shoot guns, drink beer, and eat steak as far away from their nagging wives as they could get.

Gizmo jogged up to a shorter man and whispered something into his ear. The sun gleamed off the shorter man's shaved head. His tee-shirt and tan shorts suggested that he didn't get off on playing soldier. *Jake.* Information blooped up to the surface of her consciousness. Kirk's friend. Lesley loosened a notch further. Jake owned this land. Jake was the leader of these men.

Kirk and Jake, hanging out one night listening to records … the memory she'd gleaned from Kirk clarified, and she glimpsed the old wooden console, and she heard the warm analog sound from the massive stereo system, really a piece of seventies-style furniture … two buddies smoking a little pot and downing a few cold ones. Kirk had confessed his feelings for Lesley to Jake. Lesley flinched. She gritted her teeth and shoved that away … the point was, Kirk had been one hundred percent sure that Jake would look out for her. The others might strike roughneck poses, but Jake wouldn't let anything bad happen to her.

Jake strode towards the passenger window. Large freckles dotted his bare skull. A thick reddish-blonde mustache engulfed his upper lip. His plain gray tee-shirt plastered against his sculpted pecs and his modest belly, which did not obscure the hard core underneath. She dredged up details concerning Jake.

"Who are you," he said.

She ignored the suspicion in his voice and focused on the musical quality of his tone. For a short time, he'd harbored aspirations of being a singer in a rock band. That's how he and Kirk had bridged the jock/stoner gap and had become fast friends. She riffled through all their shared interests, but she knew she would freak him out if she revealed her knowledge. "Kirk sent me. He said I'd be safe here for a few days."

Gizmo blurted, "Who's after you?"

Lesley regarded the bony, wannabe hardass. Greasy shoots of gray-tinged black hair stuck out of the back of his cap. Nothing new came to her from Kirk's intel, but *asshole* echoed. She guessed that's all she needed to know about Gizmo. She decided to tell most of the truth. "I don't know."

Gizmo jabbed his assault rifle towards the Subaru's back seat and said, "What's that? What're you tryin' to sneak into our camp?"

Lesley shifted her gaze to Jake. "I'm Lesley." She searched for an explanation, and settled on another chunk of the truth. "I took something from the museum. Bad people are trying to steal it."

Jake gave her a long look. He said to the others, "Kirk wouldn't have sent her here if it wasn't important."

Somebody at the back said, "Now wait a goddamned second …"

Jake herded the entire band of militiamen a good ten yards away from Lesley. She couldn't make out their exact words, but their general tone came through loud and clear. Gizmo spearheaded the faction that wanted her gone. She guessed they were afraid the staties, maybe even the feds, might show up with search warrants. Probably they had pot stashed on the grounds. Almost certainly some of the weapons were illegal. They might have all sorts of felony-level crap stowed in the cabin.

Jake broke away from the huddle and approached Lesley. She read the compromise in his apologetic eyes even before he said, "You gotta show what you got or the fellas won't have you."

The rest of the militia filed around the Subaru. Lesley drummed her fingertips on the steering wheel, then let her hands drop to her lap. They shouldn't see any value in a mummy. She waved a hand towards the back door. "It's unlocked."

Gizmo jerked the door open and whisked away the afghan. For a few heavy heartbeats, nobody said a word. Then Gizmo whispered, "Jesus fuckin' Christ! That's the Rewrapped Mummy!"

Chapter Three

Kirk puffed the itchy cloth away from his mouth. The black hood made his face feverish. Sweat trickled down from his temples. The hood's material obstructed just enough air to keep him on the verge of gasping.

He squirmed his bound ankles in order to get some blooding flowing in his tingling hamstrings. He drew his knees up toward his chest then stretched his legs back out along the truck's wooden floor. All through the motion he took great pains not to jostle his bound wrists. The coarse rope ate into his skin, causing a constant throb. He hated to think of his fingers going all purple. He wriggled them to make sure they hadn't gone dead. The wall's hard metal pressing into his spine assured him that they'd stowed him in the back of a moving truck. Probably they had it ready to transport the mummy, sarcophagus and all.

He blinked, then winced. His eyes felt dry as dust. Each blink seemed like razorblades scraping over his eyeballs. The constant hum of the tires on pavement had lulled him into a groggy half-sleep. He was so damned tired. He had no idea how far they'd traveled. He imagined they'd parked the truck in some remote spot in the wooded hills. He'd heard nothing but birdsong for what seemed like hours.

He gritted his teeth while riding out the urge to try to free his hands again. He bet if he rolled around, he'd find some sharp edge to slice the rope, or at least the line that connected the bonds on his wrists and ankles. Probably they'd locked him in, but at least he'd be able to reach the knot at the back of his neck and get the damned hood off his head. If he could see, he might figure out a way to escape. Or maybe he could jump them when they opened the door and make a run for it. By the end of the day he could catch up with Lesley. She must have escaped, or they wouldn't bother holding him.

He narrowed his eyes. Maybe they were taking so long because they wanted him to escape. Maybe they wanted him to lead them straight to Lesley. He set his jaw. He'd rather die. He wouldn't tell them a goddamned thing. His right eyelid fluttered, irritating his eyeball. He might never experience that insight, that bursting of the bubble that he'd always suspected he needed to become a musical genius. He might never see her again.

A faint crunching noise captured his attention. The volume of the footsteps on gravel grew. The crunching stopped outside the truck. Clanking indicated somebody fiddling with door latch. The door squeaked open. The darkness behind the hood lightened a few shades. Somebody stepped up into the truck, the force of their lunge causing a slight rocking. The door slammed shut and the darkness returned to its former blackness.

Footsteps scritched over the gritty floor towards him. "Don't move." He felt fingers at the back of his neck, working at the cord cinching the hood. The hood loosened. The material grazed his skin and mussed his hair as it slid off of him. Kirk blinked past the pain, until he worked up enough moisture in his eyes to adjust to the gloom. A thin man, the bill of his dark cap pulled down low over his forehead, a bandana wrapped around his face just below his eyes, dropped the black hood on the floor next to his boots. The masked man's windbreaker and jeans bagged around his slender frame.

The masked man lowered his head, angling his deep set eyes at Kirk. He raised his forearms and tented his spidery fingers before his chest. "Where did they go?"

Kirk couldn't place the man's accent. Kind of sounded like Indian, with that English vibe, but the sound was different, clearer, less singsong, maybe Middle Eastern.

The masked man clasped his fingers and dropped his hands to belly level. "We mean her no harm. We only desire to take possession of *it*."

The bottom dropped out of Kirk's stomach. He'd assumed their intentions, but to hear it out loud … these thieves meant to take the mummy away forever.

The man cocked his head to the left. "And, I suppose, so do you."

The sudden dryness of Kirk's mouth shriveled his attempt at a denial.

"I know that there is no need to convince you of its supernatural properties," the masked man said. "But there is a need to convince you of its true nature. We only seek to obtain it in order to destroy it. You see, it is evil."

Kirk tried to scoff, but he only managed a weak cough.

The man opened his hands, palms up. "Do you not see? It has promised you that all your wishes shall come true. Does that not seem too good to be true, to you? I believe you are far more intelligent than that."

Kirk swayed a few inches forward. He stared into the man's rich brown eyes. He saw no signs of lying. Kirk leaned back against the metal wall. His swirling thoughts threatened to accelerate into another staticky headrush.

"It used you," the masked man said. "Just as it has used every person with the bad fortune to come into contact with it."

Kirk jerked. He seized on that piece of solid ground. "The mummy is a fraud. I know all about its history."

"That history is a fraud. Perpetrated by it in order to hide from those who knew the truth, from those who would obliterate it. The archeologists who discovered it only did so because it allowed them to do so. The con artists who transported it across Europe did so because it willed them to go exactly where it wished to go. Everyone, *everyone*, who ever came into contact with it met a horrific end. If you doubt me, examine your own case."

Kirk glared at the masked man. "Then what is it?"

"It knew precisely how to manipulate you. Given how you have dedicated your life to music, it must have enticed you with the gift of sublime musical genius."

Kirk snapped his slack jaw shut. A pang for that evaporating genius shook through his chest. It had been too profound to be a trick. He'd do anything to feel it again. He knew he surely was not long for this world, knowing that such a thing existed, yet was denied to him.

"It peered into your innermost heart in order to seduce you," the masked man said. "Certainly you found your new insights exhilarating, but since you have served your purpose, and you are no longer useful to it, all that brilliance has vanished, leaving behind nothing but the ache to return to that state of grace. Now, you will do anything for it, endure anything for it. Left to your own devices, you would run to it. The sole reason we simply didn't set you free and follow you is that it has handled such attempts in the past by melting the consciousness of those unfortunate souls."

"Melting …?"

"The bdelugma has undoubtedly had a similar affect on Miss Bosh."

"The what?"

"And just as in the past, it blinds her to its true purposes, as it uses her to transport it wherever it wishes to go, in order to further its aim, which is nothing less than total destruction of the order we humans have created."

Kirk took pains not to laugh in the lunatic's face. The masked man was obviously nuts. But mocking him could set the maniac off, put him in the mood for torture.

The masked man tucked his left hand behind his back. He performed a slow swing of his right across his body while saying, "It has seduced Miss Bosh through her desire to make her little museum prestigious. World-renowned. And as a result, make herself celebrated, albeit in rarified circles."

Kirk lowered his gaze to the tips of his boots. He knew that was pure bullshit. When they were connected through the mummy, Lesley's burning desire to protect the mummy overwhelmed almost everything else, but her true feelings about the museum, that she felt obligated by her family and that she wished more than anything to get out of her joyless duty, had seeped through. The lunatic was lying.

"Are you sufficiently self-aware," the masked man said, "have you been out of the mummy's sphere of influence long enough, to realize that your depth of feeling for Miss Bosh intensified when it arrived, because it prised out of you that it could use your affection for her for its own purposes?"

Kirk's face burned.

"Ask yourself," the masked man said, "if, when it arrived, your love exploded far beyond its former state, and ask yourself if that profound explosion persists. Know that it does, because such insanity serves its purpose. This exaggerated love prevents you from committing what you perceive as a massive betrayal. No man is stronger than when he fights for all-consuming love."

Kirk stammered. He managed to silence himself before his stammer could disintegrate into full-blown babble.

"Just as in your case, as soon as she is no longer useful to it, it will discard her. You possess a unique insight into how she will feel when this happens. The emotional trauma of the inevitable separation will drive her to suicide. You know this."

Kirk raised his head and met the masked man's stare. He wanted to argue against the man, but he couldn't find any solid footing to start.

"Will you help us save her? Will you tell us where she went?"

Kirk bit down on the tip of his tongue. He teetered on the brink of spilling the beans. He latched onto the lie the masked man told about Lesley's innermost desire. He shook his head.

The masked man straightened himself out of his stoop. "I realize you have much to process. I shall give you some time to consider whether or not you wish to help us save the world, and to save the woman you love."

The masked man picked up the hood. He refitted the hood over Kirk's head and cinched it tight. "As I said, I do not believe in the efficacy of torture. But time constraints may force our hand."

The masked man's footsteps decayed away from Kirk. Light flashed and died with the opening and locking of the doors. Gravel crunched into the distance, to wherever they would decide how to get the information they wanted.

Kirk exhaled, but his muscles remained taut. He doubted he could withstand any kind of torture. He drew his knees up and inward. He would betray her. His guts cramped. He lowered his legs and let out a growling whine until the contraction relaxed. The masked man was wrong. He'd loved Lesley before the mummy arrived at the museum. He scowled. He knew he had. Wasn't just a crush, wasn't just because Lesley was so different from the girls he usually met. *Right?*

He twisted his wrists against the rough rope. He strained until the pain raged white hot and incinerated every thought and every doubt in his head. He collapsed against the metal wall and panted. They were bluffing. The masked man's lie proved he didn't know shit. All this hood and torture bullshit was just an attempt to fool him into thinking they were hardasses. By now, they must've thought they'd have the mummy, so they were freaking out.

He tapped the back of his skull against the wall. But they knew about the mummy reanimating. Maybe they were for real, maybe they were only assuming, and not lying, about Lesley. If he resisted, maybe they would torture him. He ground the back of his skull against the metal wall until his head hurt, then he stopped. They might be telling the truth. For sure the mummy could put Lesley in danger.

He tipped over onto his side. He scuffed his knees up to his belly. If he fucked this up, Lesley would pay for it. If he fucked this up, he'd never experience that musical brilliance that had already almost totally evaporated. Lesley would never forgive him if they took the mummy away from her. A deep, low sob burst out of him. He'd lose any chance he might've had with her.

Get a grip. He levered himself up into sitting position. He had to show her that he was more than just a janitor, that he was an artist, and he needed the mummy to rise to those heights. Maybe he could strike a deal, the information they wanted for access to the mummy. Long enough to reach a state of permanent genius. And for Lesley too, who had to be experiencing the same sort of thing. He grimaced. But if they fucked him, he'd lose the only thing that made life worth living.

Chapter Four

Lesley hovered around the men as they slid the mummy out of the Subaru's back seat. The side of her foot chocked into the ankle of one of the bearers. He lurched, caught his balance, and glared at Lesley. She backed several paces away from them. The tough grass stalks jabbed her bare soles. She halted. She smoothed her blue dress. She distracted herself with the reminder to ask Jake about borrowing some clothes and footwear.

The men laid the mummy on an olive army blanket. The plastic sheeting between the blanket and the grass crackled. The harsh sunlight revealed gray spots mottling some of the creases of the mummy's bandages. She needed a closer look to determine whether the spots were evidence of mold or disintegration. The mummy's clove and cumin aroma filled the camp. She couldn't believe nobody had yet mentioned anything about the pungent scent. Maybe their collective gaminess overwhelmed their sense of smell. Or maybe only she could smell it, on account of her special connection with the mummy.

The men folded the blanket around the mummy from the neck down. A man took up each corner of the plastic sheeting, which spread long enough to encase the mummy's head. She took a half step forward. She didn't know if the mummy needed to breathe. If he did, once he started suffocating, he would move. Her gaze swept over the men, pausing on Jake, then Gizmo. These men would surely freak out if the mummy showed any signs of life. She said, "Keep the head open … I'm worried about moisture being trapped …"

Gizmo contorted his thin lips. "You guys feel that? I feel weird, I'll be right back." He loped toward the main cabin.

Jake sidled up next to Lesley. His soft snort ruffled the fringes of his reddish mustache. After Gizmo entered the moss-splotched cabin, he murmured, "He's acting nuttier than usual. Maybe we should leave the camp."

Lesley shielded her eyes against the sunlight gleaming off of Jake's shaved skull. "Where would we go?"

"I have an island."

Lesley cocked her head.

Jake's brown eyes twinkled. "Sounds highfalutin', I know. Basically just a rock off the coast, some trees, been in the family since forever. But it's easily defended by just a few guys. I'll pick some men we can trust, and then you can figure out your next move."

"Yes," Lesley said. "I think that might be for the best."

Jake strode towards the mummy. "Wrap it up boys, and put it in the back of my truck." He twisted toward Lesley and said, "We'll gas you up and you can follow me there."

Lesley cupped her left fist in her right palm and squeezed. She chastised herself for her quick, unconsidered agreement. Jake supervised his men, directing them to begin swathing plastic around the mummy at the feet. He could lose her on the back roads. One of his men could tamper with her car. Or they could just take the mummy. She couldn't stop them if they tried. She swallowed the lump in her throat. She said, "I'd better leave Kirk's car here. The police might be looking for it by now. I should ride with you."

Jake didn't turn his head but he flicked his eyes to their corners. Lesley gripped her fist tighter. He gave her a terse nod. Lesley relaxed a smidge. The island sounded good. A place where she could settle down and let the mummy open up to her, like she knew he would. Just the knowledge of how he was able to reanimate was sure to revolution medicinal science. She would let others deal with the applications, whether in the fields of health, even energy … the implications for solving the world's big problems seemed endless. The mummy had chosen her as his conduit. She had to be careful about letting Jake and his followers in on this.

The four men, arraying themselves at the head and feet of the mummy, counted, in unison, "One, two, three," and on three, they lifted the mummy off of the grass. They toted the mummy towards the open canopy of Jake's big blue truck.

Gizmo came galloping out of the cabin towards the men. A black riot helmet and its tinted visor disguised his head and face, but Lesley recognized his gangly limbs. The confines of the helmet hollowed out his voice as he blurted, "Whoa whoa whoa, what's going on?"

A couple of the loiterers stepped up, chuckling. Another guy said, "What's with the get-up?"

Gizmo skidded to a stop between the men carrying the mummy and the open tailgate of Jake's truck. Gizmo said, "You can't smell that?"

Lesley squeezed her fist with her palm until it hurt. She released her fist. She narrowed her eyes at Gizmo. He might've detected the life in the mummy.

"Where you taking it?" Gizmo said.

Jake planted his hands on his hips. His tee-shirt and khaki shorts made his macho pose look kind of like an overgrown boy playing tough-guy. His firm tone however, bolstered her, when he said, "To the island."

Gizmo surveyed the rest of the men, who gathered around the little dustup, then said, "You all need to put your helmets on too. This thing fucks with people's minds."

Lesley winced. Three of the guys broke away from the pack and trotted to the cabin. The men carrying the mummy set him down on the grass. Two of them headed towards the barracks.

Jake circled back around to Lesley. He mumbled, "We got some special helmets, protects against long-range acoustic weapons, that sort of thing."

Gizmo jabbed a bony finger at the stragglers and said, in a singsong tone, "You'll be sorry ..."

His warning prompted two more to hurry toward the barracks. Jake stood his ground. Out of the side of his mouth he said to Lesley, "You seem all right. You have any reason to think he's onto something?"

Lesley heard the lie in her voice as she said, "It's a museum exhibit."

"Then why are they trying to steal it?" Gizmo said. "And why are you trying to stop them? Why didn't you call the cops?"

Lesley opened her mouth, but she couldn't think of a response, before Gizmo said, "I'll tell you why. Cosimo is controlling her mind."

Lesley scoffed towards Gizmo's tinted visor. The mummy had not revealed his true name to her. She sensed that he was still debating whether or not he could trust her. Keeping him safe was the test. As far as mind control went, she thought opening her mind was far more accurate.

Jake smiled with one corner of his mouth. "Cosimo?"

"The mummy," Gizmo said, "is Cosimo Medici. The last Medici overlord before the family went underground."

"You get that from Wikipedia?" Jake asked.

Gizmo's bony shoulders tensed. His voice dropped into a chilly monotone. "No. I researched this stuff when I first heard the Rewrapped Mummy was coming to Portland. The official story is nobody knows where the mummy came from, exactly. The truth is, Cosimo was into some dark shit. His whole family had been, for centuries. That's how they held onto power for so long."

Lesley had to strain to keep from rolling her eyes. Helmeted men returned from the barracks, some with their visors down. Gizmo's story drew them to him, as he said, "Cosimo, like so many rich bastards like him, started wasting his family's resources on chasing immortality. Like the rich fucks don't have enough, they want to live forever too."

The more fervent members of his audience sneered their agreement. Jake shrugged and said, "Of course."

Lesley crossed her arms over her chest. She'd fallen in with conspiracy theorists, apocalypse-preparedness types. She did the math. Whoever concocted this cockamamy story got the timeline more or less correct. Of course, the truth was a million miles away from Gizmo's rumors.

One of Gizmo's helmeted faction said, "Are you sayin' this is some magic-type bullshit?"

Gizmo, over the rising chuckles from Jake's tee-shirt-and-shorts cronies, blurted, "NO!" The chuckles stopped dead. Gizmo puffed up his scrawny chest. He pointed his finger in the air and said, "But enough people believe to make them do some crazy shit. Like the crazy fuckers chasing her." Gizmo stabbed his finger towards Lesley.

"If you don't believe," Jake said, "why the helmet and the mask?"

Lesley, even though the helmet hid Gizmo's face, thought she saw rage in the trembles that rippled through Gizmo's long frame. She read more than a little alpha-male posturing in Jake's straight spine. The schism in the camp became crystal clear.

"I'm not sayin' it's magic," Gizmo said. "I'm sayin' it's chemicals. You gotta be able to smell that."

The men quieted. Jake's smirk vanished under his moustache. Gizmo swelled. Lesley shook off a shimmer of trepidation. Her connection to the mummy, she couldn't explain it to these men. They wouldn't believe her if she did … or maybe they would and they would seize the mummy for themselves. She didn't doubt that these men would experience some kind of overflow, some kind of ambient affect of her connection to the mummy.

"But that don't mean there ain't whackos that think old Cosimo hit on some real, honest to god magic." Gizmo kicked his toe toward the mummy and said, "Shit, there's cults that worship this fucking thing. Some of 'em think this here is Jesus in the flesh, about to rise from the dead again any day now." His visored face revolved toward Lesley. "That's why she came to us instead of the cops. One of those batshit crazy cults is on her tail."

Lesley did her level best to maintain her composure against the stirring anxiety within, but a sweat droplet trickled from her temple down to her jaw. The urge to brush the sweat away drove her up the wall. She remained still, just to deny him the satisfaction of witnessing a guilty gesture.

A slight waggle disturbed Gizmo's helmet. *He knows.* The swirling inside Lesley raged into a hurricane. She bit down on her tongue in order to maintain her calm demeanor. He knew that the mummy was animate. She didn't know how, maybe he was more sensitive than the others, maybe the ambient mental flow between her and the mummy, the overflow, had spilled into him more than the others, and by sheer accident he'd realized the truth. If so, he would want the mummy for himself.

"Should've had better security," Gizmo said. "Should've know better. See, the whole point of the tour was to drive up the price. Some consortium of lawyers and bankers colluded to sue for ownership, and they got it. Took over ten years, but they finally ground down everybody else with a legal claim, ran them out of money. So they needed to drum up publicity, to drive the price up, recoup their investment." Gizmo raised his index finger. "But not how you think. See, they announce the tour, they insure the shit out it, every kind of policy they can get their greedy hands on. Meanwhile, they strike a deal with the cult with the deepest pockets. But they don't hand old Cosimo over, oh no. They book a stop on the tour at some rinky-dink museum in a remote, underpopulated area. And if you don't think Portland fills the bill, you best think again. Then they sell the cult all the info you guys supplied them. Floor plans, security details, all that shit."

Lesley felt his point like a kick in the guts. Still, she maintained her outward calm. But he was right about that much. The ownership group had demanded all those details, and she had happily provided them, before any contracts were signed. And the cult's squad had known exactly when to hit when there'd be the fewest people in the building. Sure, they could've waited till the wee hours, when the building was deserted, but, she imagined, with their windbreakers and jeans, they intended to look like ordinary workmen if any cops should happen by, a ploy which wouldn't fly at three in the morning. And his point about the museum landing such a prestigious exhibit … it all made sense.

"That way," Gizmo said, "they get paid twice, by the insurance companies and under the table by the cult. Hell, they might even sue your museum, end up owning that too."

A wave of nausea threatened to spoil Lesley's composure. She'd bet anything she looked a little green in the gills.

"Tell you what," Gizmo said to Lesley. "Ain't none of them gonna be too damned happy with you." The other men nodded and grumbled their assent. "The bankers might still get their insurance money, but they gonna have some *very* unhappy customers. Both sides'll probably do anything to get their property back." His visor tilted an inch to the left. "You think murder's out of the question?"

She bit down harder on her tongue. They might murder Kirk. They might've already.

In the dead silence, Gizmo leaned forward, and he laced his voice with a sinister tone while saying, "Old Cosimo here's been making folks murder each other for at least a couple hundred years. You gotta know that. Only a dumbass would think anything's different now."

Lesley stared into his inky visor. She couldn't see his face at all, but her every nerve ending sent danger signals to her brain. If he got the chance, the temptation to murder her might prove overwhelming for this man. Since he *knew*. She couldn't fathom what sort of affect the mummy might have on a twisted mind. She watched his visor shift from centered on her, to centered on Jake, and back again. She interpreted that move to mean that only Jake stood between her and death.

"Probably be better for you if you just turn Cosimo over to us," Gizmo said. "Just for safekeeping."

Lesley recognized that she'd bared her teeth. She willed her lips to close.

"I got a safer place than Jake's island," Gizmo said. "Why don't you stuff him in the back of my truck, and all your worries'll be behind you."

"Now hold on," Jake said. "This is still America, and we're still Americans. We don't go taking other folks' property."

Gizmo's visor zeroed in on Jake. His entire helmet seemed to vibrate. Lesley swore she could feel the pure hatred sizzling towards Jake, whose comrades closed ranks around him.

"Now I agree we gotta get it out of the camp," Jake said. "Least ways before the feds show up, or these cults, or whoever. But my friend sent her here for protection, and I owe him. If she wants to take off alone, that's her business. But if she wants our help, my island is a helluva lot better than that hole in your backyard that you call a 'bunker,' that ain't gonna be worth spit when the chips are down anyways. So I say it's her call."

Lesley studied Jake. His brown eyes rounded into a kindness that just couldn't be authentic. She couldn't trust any of them. But the cult could show up at any second, and they could get away with whatever they wanted to do out here in the middle of nowhere. At least with Jake's plan, they'd see them coming. She said, "The island sounds good to me."

Jake nodded. "You heard the lady, load him up. Harry, get my go-bag, will ya?"

"Hold up," Gizmo said. "We all oughtta go. "For protection. We don't know how many they might come with."

"If they come," Jake said.

"If they come," Gizmo mocked, "you're gonna need all hands on deck."

Lesley couldn't think of an argument against Gizmo. Jake said, "Okay. Everybody, load up."

Lesley said to Jake, "We should leave somebody, in case Kirk shows up."

Jake sucked his teeth. He said, "And somebody who won't talk about the island in case the bad guys show up." Jake pointed to a squat, bearded young man. "Terrell, you stay, man the camp."

"Sure boss," Terrell said.

"All right then," Jake said. "Let's saddle up!"

The men, both the helmeted and Jake's faction, hopped to it. Gizmo and Jake engaged in a brief staredown. Maybe the two of them would counterbalance each other, give her enough time on this island to show them what her, *her*, connection to the mummy could do for the world. These men were dissatisfied with the world and wanted change, after all, or they wouldn't be playing soldier in the middle of the woods.

She squared her shoulders and strode forward to supervise the men moving the mummy into Jake's truck.

Chapter Five

A sharp clank startled Kirk. His involuntary twitch irritated his raw wrists. He drew his outstretched legs toward himself, his jeans scraping against the dirty wooden floorboards, then a hamstring cramp forced him to straighten them again. Under the hood, the blackness lightened a few shades. The clomps approaching him caused the trailer to jounce on its shocks. Each slight bounce hurt his wounded wrists. He suppressed his reaction down to a clenched hiss. He didn't want to give his tormenter the satisfaction.

The footsteps stopped in front of him. He sensed the interrogator's hesitation. He inhaled the sourness of his own sweat and breath, which saturated the damp fabric. Maybe the man was working up the nerve for murder. The hood ruffled off of his head. Kirk blinked, trying to adjust his eyes.

The lone man said, in a no-nonsense, American accident, "We caught Miss Bosh. She won't tell us where she hid it. You tell us, or we will kill her."

Kirk closed his eyes. No way would she ever leave the mummy. The bastard was lying. That meant that they hadn't found her. The tension drained out of his jaw and shoulders. All he had to do was escape. Then he would hook up with Lesley, and the mummy, and he'd get it all back. A smile ghosted across his cracked lips.

The man's tone went sarcastic as he said, "I told them you'd see right through that one. But I got outvoted." He squatted down to eye level with Kirk. "Let's get real. The effects of the bdelugma must be starting to wear off by now."

Kirk looked the man up and down. The same dark bandana up to his eyes, and the same hat with the bill pulled down low as the first guy. The same windbreaker and jeans did not disguise this man's thicker, brawler's body. Probably they decided to send in their badass to intimidate him, and to convince him that his feelings for Lesley were bullshit. He sought the tattered ends of his connection to Lesley and came up with nothing. He winced. He knew his feelings were real. He remembered how he felt before the mummy, before the bdela-whatever.

"You must be in deep emotional pain," the masked man said. "Since the euphoria you felt in its presence must be long gone."

Kirk slumped. He closed his eyes. He couldn't argue against the man. The absence of that insight made him feel hollow, shriveled. He suppressed a cough that he feared would tear up his dry throat.

"If you don't talk," the man said, "you'll never experience it again. That's a stone-cold fact."

The words surged up into his mouth, the rush catching Kirk off guard, but he managed to clamp his teeth together and swallow his confession, which became a weak tremble across his lips

"I'm not gonna go over the trail of blood and misery it has left behind it," the man said. "I'm not gonna try to convince you that it is bent on the total destruction of all humanity. Even though those things are true. The thing you gotta ask yourself, do you think we're the only ones who know the truth?"

Kirk opened his eyes. The bill of the crouching man's hat shadowed his gaze.

"Even if you don't believe us," the man said, "you think there aren't other people out looking for her right now? Some of them are very bad people."

"Not like you, right?" Kirk choked down another cough. Speaking threatened to bloody his dry throat.

"Some of them believe other things," the man said. "Others believe the same thing we do, only they want to bring it on. Shit'll go very bad for her if they find her. The best thing for everybody, and I mean everybody, is you tell us where she is, so maybe we can get to her before anybody else does."

Kirk sniffed. He regretted the quiet inhale. He didn't want to give the man any sign of wavering. *I'm not wavering*! He wasn't about to fall for their line of bullshit.

"I know you'll want proof that we are who we say we are." The man shifted from his crouch down to one knee, next to a small black case that had escaped Kirk's notice. "You might think that we're bluffing, since we've given you so much time to come to your senses." He laid the case on its side and flicked open the pair of clasps. "You might think that if the stakes are so goddamned high, these crazy people would've hurt me by now." He raised the lid until it locked perpendicular to its bottom. "Let the fact that we haven't hurt you be your proof that we're not bad men." He spun the case around. Snug in the black foam padding, a sleek cordless drill and a half dozen nasty bits gleamed in the hazy light.

Kirk struggled to catch his breath.

"We're not bad men," the American said. "But you're making us desperate men." His knee joints crackled as he stood up. "Don't think you can just wait us out. We aren't gonna just let you walk away if we don't get what we want from you. Some of the boys want to fuck you up just to teach you a lesson. And the next guy that talks to you might not be so nice."

The man marched to the other end of the trailer and jumped outside. The door slammed shut. The drill still gleamed in the deeper darkness. They knew that music was his life. They would go after his fingers. Then his eyes. He shuddered. He figured he'd spill his guts if they just nicked one of his knuckles with a whirring bit.

He looked toward the doors. He couldn't see how something that could make him soar like he had, when he was connected to her, when he was immersed in those stunning epiphanies ... he had no inkling that it was possible to feel that ... *joyful*, and he couldn't see how the mummy could make him feel that way, and be evil at the same time. He flared his nostrils and slitted his eyelids. He could definitely see human beings lying, no fucking problem. But the man's claim that other groups were looking for Lesley, that rang true. And it sounded right that if he didn't help them, they weren't gonna just let him go.

Moisture shimmered his vision. The threat of tears shocked him. He whispered, "Good." He'd rather die than never experience that joy again. His chest hitched. He willed his mind towards Lesley. His eyes dried. She was in danger. They were gonna torture him if he didn't tell them what he knew. But if by some miracle he managed to withstand them, she might be worse off than she was now. And they might be telling the truth, after everything else.

He tried to pull his wrists apart. The ropes bit into his wounds. The pain sizzled white hot through his brain. He stifled a cry. He dropped his throbbing hands into his lap. His head sagged, his chin touching his chest.

Chapter Six

Lesley jerked out of a nod. She grabbed the edge of the tailgate to prevent herself from falling out of Jake's truck. She slid an inch back onto the cool metal. She pulled the hem of the tee shirt out from under her ass. At least the baggy shirt and fatigue pants were clean. She wasn't sure about the combat boots, which ranged enough sizes too big so that they threatened to slip off her dangling feet and clop to the dirt.

She yawned till her jaw popped. She gazed over the dark waters and began the calculation of how long she'd gone without sleep, at least twenty-four hours, but the simple math wore her down before she could complete the work.

She rubbed her eyes. She focused on Jake's private dock. The simple construction of pilings and planks extended a good distance from the rocky coastline into the ocean. Normally Jake kept his boat here, but some buddy of his was rebuilding something or other, she didn't quite remember his explanation for the boat's absence. Jake had assured her that a trusted friend, piloting his fishing trawler, was on the way. Going by the number of micronaps she'd slipped into, she calculated that friend was supposed to be here maybe two hours ago.

She inhaled a lungful of spicy aroma. She twisted and pulled the blanket a little more below the mummy's chin. She studied him for any signs of life. She couldn't be certain outside of her lab, but she believed the spots around the windings' creases were stress marks from the mummy's movements. She exhaled. Maybe. Maybe she was interpreting the evidence so that it fit into her delusion. Maybe the mummy never moved.

The metallic *pop* and carbonated hiss of an opened beer can focused her stare on the pack of men dawdling around Gizmo's truck, which Gizmo had parked next to the treeline, just far enough away so that Lesley heard their conspiring voices, but couldn't make out their words. The darkness transformed their helmets into silhouettes of shamanesque masks, the lifted visors reminding her of representations of sacred birds. Jake's partisans huddled around the front end of Jake's truck, Jake himself sitting in his cab, murmuring to the others. One of his guys called towards Gizmo's men, saying, "Don't be an asshole."

Lesley zeroed in on the beer drinker, one of Gizmo's crew, as he bellowed, "What? Gotta kill the time someway."

"Gotta stay sharp! This ain't war games, this is for real!" Lesley shifted toward the protester, who stomped across the sandy soil between the two factions. A few of his comrades backed him up.

She searched for Jake's bald skull among the converging men. She spotted Gizmo's lanky frame, his helmet bobbing a half-head higher than everybody else. The helmets made Gizmo's goons seem taller and more sinister than Jake's average-sized men. Somebody cracked open another beer, then another, and she saw a helmeted man thrust a beer into the face of a bare-headed man, and one handed, he opened the can and a mist of foam sprayed into the glower of the bare-headed man, who slapped the can out of the helmeted man's hand. The two groups surged into each other. Growls and smacks of flesh against flesh resounded out of the dark scrum.

Jake, his voice ringing out, said, "Enough!"

The groups parted. Jake stood in the middle, his arms outstretched towards each faction. He pointed toward his men and said, "Holster those firearms!"

Lesley scanned the dark tangle of limbs and torsos. She didn't see any drawn guns.

A slight warble spoiled Gizmo's toughguy tone as he said, "Stand down!"

"Once we get to the island you fellas can chill out," Jake said. "In *shifts*. But until then, we're all on high alert. Got it?" Jake elevated his voice over the sheepish mumbles, saying, "Got it?"

Somebody broke the silence, saying, "They ain't gonna show, anyways."

"S'posed to be here two hours ago."

Lesley clamped her teeth together. They might be right.

Gizmo, his voice steadying, said, "Maybe its time we take Cosimo to my bunker. Secure the package and plan the next move."

Lesley focused her glare on Gizmo. He had to get Jake out of the way before he could steal the mummy. She was afraid that Jake didn't understand the threat, that he hadn't noticed that Gizmo's schemes had grown into an obsession. She'd noticed however. The sly looks. The persistent licking of his lips. The long stares, when he had his visor down, thinking nobody knew, but she knew, oh, she knew. Probably Jake was used to dealing with Gizmo's attempts to make himself important, and that habit had dulled his faculties. The stakes were different now, higher. Gizmo *knew*. Probably he didn't know exactly, but he had intuited enough. On the bright side, this meant that, probably, she wasn't insane.

"He would've called if he wasn't coming," Jake said. He looked towards Lesley, then faced Gizmo. "We settled this. We wait."

Lesley caught herself squeezing her fist again. She relaxed as much as she was able. There was nothing to do but wait, but she couldn't help feeling that with each passing second, the cult was catching up to her. She winced. She shoved the possibilities of what they might have inflicted on poor Kirk out of her mind. She had no choice. She had to leave him behind.

"We ain't gonna wait all night," Gizmo said.

"We won't," Jake said. "If he doesn't show, we go to Plan B."

Lesley studied Jake. They hadn't discussed a Plan B. She narrowed her eyes. He drove here, a few feet away from the mummy. Perhaps some psychic overflow had affected him too. Perhaps he had his own designs on the mummy.

She drew her legs up and crossed them Indian-style while rotating towards Jake. She reached behind herself and caressed the plastic over the mummy's ankle. She took a deep breath and her heartbeat slowed. She gazed over the water. A light flickered in the distance. Her vision blurred. The men's realization of the boat's approach fazed down to a minor hiss. Soon they would get to the island. Soon she and the mummy would get to work.

"Ah Christ," Jake said.

Lesley refocused on the boat, which seemed to struggle lower in the water than it should. She didn't know boats, but as the craft neared, she thought the rigging shouldn't be so snarled. The darkness didn't hide the stains and crust scrimming the hull.

Gizmo shouted, "Hooty hoo hoo hoo!"

Jake circled to the other side of the tailgate.

"Is there a problem?" Lesley said.

Jake crawled onto the tailgate and into the canopy. His weight rocked the truck. "My friend must've not been able to make it. He sent his cousin Cliff instead. Cliff's an asshole." Jake covered up the face of the mummy with the flap of the blanket. "He's one of Gizmo's running buddies. He can't be trusted."

Lesley squeezed her right fist. She had to, to keep herself from pulling the blanket away from the mummy's face. She scrutinized the mummy for any evidence of motion, of suffocation.

Jake slid out of the canopy. He strode towards the men, barking orders. Some scrambled onto the dock, others came toward the truck. Lesley uncrossed her legs and swung off the tailgate. Her too-big boots clomped onto the soil. She made way for the crew, but supervised their work as they eased the mummy out of the truck. Lesley accompanied the crew to the dock. The urge to whisk the blanket away from the mummy's head nearly drove her crazy.

"Hold up cowboy!"

Lesley halted with the crew. She turned toward the source of that cigarette-harshed voice. A large man scaled down a ladder hanging along the boat's side. A few rungs above the dock, the large man leapt off the ladder. His landing shook the dock. His shoulders seemed twice as broad as his hips. He pulled off his ballcap. He ran his hand over his forehead and through his long dark stringy hair, then tucked his cap back on his bulky head. His steroid-suspicious body blocked Jake from leading the way up the little ramp to the boat's deck. He said, "Whatcha got there, boss?"

"I cleared everything with Dean," Jake said.

"Well Dean ain't the cap-ee-tan for this little nighttime voyage. You got drugs, guns, or is it a fucking corpse, like it looks like?"

Lesley saw Jake bristle. Jake said, "Cliff ..."

Cliff jabbed his index finger in Jake's face. "Call me *Captain*."

Gizmo, already aboard, snickered.

Cliff shifted his attention from Jake to Lesley. He looked her up and down, his leer lingering first at her hips, then at her breasts. Heat surged into Lesley's face. Cliff said, "Who's she?"

Lesley crossed her arms over her chest. She curled her fingers into fists. She envisioned the whole crime at once. Gizmo, Cliff, and the helmeted faction overwhelming Jake and his small contingent. Then the rape, the murder, and the dumping of her body at sea.

"*Captain*," Jake said, "we've got a burial to perform on the island."

Despite the darkness, despite the bill of his cap shading his face, Lesley read Cliff's assumptions as he gaped at Lesley, then at the corpse. Throw in a sketchy trip to an island in the middle of the night, and he had to believe that Lesley had murdered somebody.

Cliff looked up at Gizmo. Lesley missed whatever sign Gizmo gave, but Cliff stepped aside and performed a sweep of his bulging arm. "You have permission to board."

The men carried the mummy on board. Lesley followed. Gizmo had pulled Cliff aside. She couldn't make sense of his whispers, but she didn't need to. The pair's conversation commanded Jake's attention too. Jake seemed to tense every muscle in his body. She hurried to the mummy's side. They were all plotting against her.

Chapter Seven

Kirk peered into the darkness, which had deepened, and engulfed the drill a while ago. He expected the crunch of gravel any second now. They would expect his decision. He reverted to the one plan he'd come up with, and tried to foresee another outcome. Crawl over and somehow turn the drill on his bonds. After freeing himself, somehow open the locked doors. Then run for it, except they'd be waiting, alerted by the noise, and they'd swarm him, bulldog him to the dirt. There was no other ending.

A series of jagged coughs tore up his dry throat. The fit shook his torso and jostled his wrists, provoking a flash of white hot pain from his rope burns. His head jerked backwards. His skull smacked into the metal wall. He gnashed his teeth through the agony, then dropped his jaw to his chest.

He snuffled in shallow breaths until the pain dulled. He could take it. For her, he could take their worst. He would spit in their faces, and make them go too far and accidentally kill him. Then she would be safe from them.

He focused on a dim glint in the darkness. Could be his eyes playing tricks on him. He sniffed and detected a hint of machine oil. His eyelids sagged to slits. They wouldn't accidentally kill him. They'd go after his fingers. They would bring lights, so he could see the bits of flesh and blood and bone flying up from the back of his hand as the drill bore through to his palm. He would never play again. He shuddered. He didn't think he could bear to pick up his guitar, anyways, with just the memory, no, not even that, just a fading impression of what he had been capable of in the mummy's presence. The critics and haters called him a hack. In the wee hours, when he couldn't fall asleep, he worried that they might be right. Now, he knew for sure. He'd been less than a speck. Next to nothing. If he couldn't get that genius back, then let them take his fucking hands.

He tried to suppress another burst of coughs, but they exploded up his ragged throat. His heaving chest rattled his wrists. The rope burns flared. For a moment, the pain overloaded his brain. He pressed his head into the wall. He arched his back, raising his ass and hamstrings off of the floor. Cramps constricted both calves. He dropped back to the wooden floor. The collision sent a fresh burst of pain sizzling up from his wrists. He drew his knees to his torso. He hunched his back. His forehead grazed his kneecaps. The agony ebbed. His calf muscles relaxed. He eased his legs to full straightness. He leaned back against the wall. He rasped, "Goddamn."

He mastered his breathing. If he didn't get some water soon, he figured he would die of thirst. At least then he wouldn't have to worry about withstanding torture. He stopped his smile partway, when his lips started to crack. He knew it was fake, anyways. Just like his will to resist. Even if these bastards had never tortured anybody before, they could look up everything they needed to know online. They were probably learning how to waterboard on Youtube even as he sat there. They were gonna break him like he was made of glass. He was gonna tell them everything they wanted to know. Then they would murder him, or, at best, leave him a broken mess, no good to anybody.

He found himself moaning. He mutated this emission into a weak growl. *Make a deal.* At least then he would be there when they caught up to her. Maybe he'd be able to save her. He nodded. He would demand that they could not harm her. He would demand time with the mummy, enough time to recapture those heights, *permanently*. And time for her too, to get what she needed. And, after everything, they could be telling the truth.

The trailer seemed to expand, to keep enlarging, so that the smallest *tick* roared in his ears. He felt like he was shrinking. He felt like if he stalled any longer, he would chicken out. "Hey!" His voice sounded tiny and rough. He cleared his throat, and yelled, "Hey!"

The effort agitated his throat. He endured another coughing jag. He lifted his hands from his lap in order to protect his raw wrists. He couldn't call out again. But he knew they heard him. This was what they'd been waiting for.

He bowed his head. He knew they were liars. He knew he loved her for real. He wouldn't hurt so bad otherwise. He hoped his yearning to recapture that musical insight wasn't clouding his mind. He didn't think so. But he had expected some clarity, some sign, some inkling that he was making the right choice. Or the wrong one. *Nothing.* He felt the same, only smaller and smaller and smaller.

Chapter Eight

A heavy splash on the other side of the cabin's wall startled Lesley. She expected a cry for help, or somebody calling, 'Man overboard!' She didn't like the quizzical look in Jake's brown eyes. The fishing boat's timbers creaked. The waves outside lapped against the hull.

"I better check it out," Jake said. He stood up and unholstered his pistol. "I don't want to leave you alone. Just in case."

Lesley gripped the underside of her seat. She did not rise from the cabin-long wooden bench. The mummy's head rested an inch from her thigh. His body stretched out over the rest of the bench. She'd unwrapped his face. She had to resist the compulsion to touch the bandages. The private cabin's dim lamplight hampered her attempts at a proper examination, but the ancient fabric seemed more sallow. She knew the salty, moist sea air would accelerate degradation. Maybe if Jake left her alone, *finally*, the mummy might reanimate and communicate what special care he might require. But if Jake left her alone, she'd be helpless should Gizmo and Cliff decide to make a move. The splash might've been their bait to separate Jake from her. She pushed up to her feet. Jake led the way out of the cramped cabin. He took a last glance at the mummy.

Lesley stared at the back of his bald head. He might just be worried about leaving the mummy unguarded too. They stepped into the mess. She scanned the low-ceilinged, cluttered room. Dirty dishes and plastic cups cluttered the long table. She'd already catalogued the filthy nooks and crannies, the peeling paint and graffiti carved into the walls. She said, "Where is everyone?"

"They must be topside."

Jake ascended the steps. Lesley felt the risers sag under her cloddy boots. Jake's shoulders brushed the walls of the chute-like stairwell. Lesley guessed a giant like Cliff had to go up crabwise while ducking.

Jake stepped toward the deck's railing. He pointed and said, "There it is." Lesley clomped up the last steps to the deck. She squinted while grasping the rail. For a moment, she saw nothing, then the darker shapes of trees manifested. The span of the forest suggested a decent-sized chunk of land, bigger than she anticipated. She leaned against the rail, shut her eyes, and exhaled. Soon she would have the peace and quiet she needed. She opened her eyes and gazed into the trees. The beginning of ... *everything*, would happen on this humble island. The world would never be the same. She filled her lungs, and exhaled again. She smiled. She couldn't wait to get started.

"You could ride out the apocalypse here," Jake said.

Lesley shifted her eyes toward Jake. He surveyed the island. She reminded herself that he was the sort of person who played soldier in the middle of the woods. She shifted back to the island. They should be safe from the cult, even if those fanatics tortured the location out of Kirk. She winced.

"Where the hell is everybody?" Jake said.

She followed his frown into a full turn. Nobody manned the deck or the rigging. "Maybe they're sleeping?"

With his thumb and forefinger, Jake stroked his mustache. "Nah, we're here. They'd be ... ready ..."

"What is it?"

"We should've started circling in to dock by now."

Lesley watched the island. She rotated her head as they came abreast trees, as Jake called out to his men, and as they passed by the trees, and as Jake's calls became more shrill. *Mistake* ... she shook her head. Cliff and Gizmo had recharted their destination.

"This is weird," Jake said. "Let's go check out the bridge."

Jake trotted beside the rail. Lesley trailed him, tugging herself hand over hand along the rail. She marveled at his surefootedness in the darkness, on which the single light, an orangish safety beacon high up in the rigging, had little affect. The smell of dead fish made her wrinkle her nose. She supposed the mummy's spicy aroma had masked the stink before. She caught up to Jake, who'd come to a standstill. He stared into the dark windows of the bridge. She might be a landlubber, but she knew that couldn't be right. She raised her hand to grab his shirt, to pull him back to the cabin before Gizmo and Cliff could steal the mummy.

He surged away from her. Her hand clutched empty air. She hurried after him, her clumsy footfalls thumping on the deck. He reached the door on the far side of the bridge. He grabbed the knob and twisted. He muttered, "Locked."

She caught up to him as he shouldered the door. He said, "I can feel something solid behind the door. I can't budge it."

She seized his elbow. "We have to get back to the mummy."

He met her gaze. "Don't you get it? We're adrift."

The whizzing of unspooling cord whipped her attention above. A mass plummeted toward her. Before she could flinch, the mass popped to a halt with the crack of snapping bone. The force of the drop tilted the boat enough to propel Lesley's hip into the railing. She yawed over the side. Her heels left the deck. Jake caught one of her ankles and yanked her back onto the deck. She fell flat on her back. She gaped up at the limp body swinging overhead. Fluid pattered to the deck a few feet away from her, tracing the pendulum pattern of the hung man.

Chapter Nine

Lesley kept her head down, and her eyes aimed at the deck, but, as the burden of the hanged man wound the line around, decelerating to maximum tension, then, accelerating, unwound, then wound the other way, again and goddamned again, the cord's creaking forced the corpse into the forefront of her mind. Jake had identified the dead man as one of Cliff's hands. They hadn't detected a sign of anyone else. She swallowed her gorge. "Somebody did this," she said. "We have to get back before they take the mummy."

Jake gave her a herky-jerky nod while muttering, "Yeah." He tottered along the railing. Lesley fell in behind him. With each step, her nausea lessened. Still, she couldn't remember if they were going around the portside or starboard. *The other side*. That was the best she could do, under the circumstances. She supposed she was suffering mild shock. She couldn't make sense of the hanged man. Way too much effort to murder someone like that, when all you had to do was throw them overboard. She recalled that heavy splash outside the cabin. Must've been someone, but thrown, or jumped? A rash of suicides made no sense at all, unless …

"What the fuck is happening to me?"

She bumped into Jake's shoulder blade. She took a backwards step. She knew by his burnt-tobacco voice before she looked over Jake's head. Cliff's hulking shape barred their way.

"Cliff," Jake said. "Where's Gizmo?"

"All, my, life," Cliff said.

The darkness, the angle, blacked out Cliff's face. His stringy hair, however, vibrated, and then she saw the erratic oscillations shaking his monstrous frame.

Cliff inhaled through his nose, the breath starting shuddery but steadying by the end. "This is some bullshit," he said. "You motherfuckers did this."

A man hurtled into Cliff and the two of them flipped over the railing. A loud whump preceded the spray which doused Lesley's head and neck. Jake flinched into Lesley. She scrambled backwards, got her feet underneath herself, and held the two of them upright. Jake snatched the rail.

A subtle footfall sounded behind Lesley. A hunched man, the darkness concealing his identity, stole towards her. He stopped. He pivoted to the rail and stared at the water.

Jake lurched toward the front of the boat. Lesley hurried after him. A hatch door whined open and two men crawled onto the deck. The stink gagged Lesley. Jake said, "Rick, what are you doing?"

Furtive noises drew Lesley's attention. She rotated in a semicircle, her backside against the railing. Men seemed to pop up all over the place, crawling over the rigging, clambering over the cabins and hatches. One man dropped from the roof of the bridge onto another man's back. He rode him down to the deck. He dug a kneecap into the downed man's spine while clasping his hands together against his victim's Adam's apple. He wrenched backwards. The downed man's bones popped.

The attacker leapt up from the downed man, who didn't move. The attacker prowled towards Lesley. "Jake," she said. "Jake!"

She half-turned towards him. Jake had drawn his gun. He chewed his lower lip. A man rushed by them, sideswiping Lesley, and collided with her would-be assailant. The two men fell overboard.

Jake grabbed her hand and tugged her behind him. She concentrated on keeping up with him. The smacks of flesh against flesh surrounded her. More heavy splashes came from the right, more men plunging into the ocean. Jake navigated through battle, leading her to the stairwell. He faced her, wide-eyed, and shouted, "Go!"

She ricocheted from wall to wall down to the deserted mess. She lunged inside the cabin and slammed the door shut behind herself. The mummy sat on the bench. The plastic wrapping and the blanket pooled around his feet. His bandaged hand patted the bench next to him. She sat down. He took both of her hands in one of his. She felt her heartbeat drop to a calm rhythm.

She stared into the bandages that swathed his face. She whispered, "What's happening?"

They'd been scheming to seize him. *She knew it.* Their plans fell apart because each man was as greedy as the next. She nodded. It was true. She forced down her fear. He needed her focused, if they were going to make it out of this, if they were going to gain control of the boat.

Chapter Ten

Kirk stared out of the front windshield and murmured, "We should've seen somebody by now." He settled back on low bench running along the back of the van. The rutted dirt road rocked the van from side to side. The van's undercarriage threshed the tall grass. Kirk rubbed the smooth white tape that pressed gauze against his injured wrists. He cleared his throat, which felt a lot better after they gave him some water, but still, he wouldn't be singing for his supper any time soon.

Kirk fixated on the Middle-Eastern man, who sat across from him. The cap low on the forehead and the bandana pulled up to his dark eyes, like the other half-dozen men in the back of the van, didn't disguise his identity. The other men he'd seen seemed like Americans. This guy carried himself like he was the boss. Kirk said, "We should've seen guards by now."

The van slowed to a stop. Kirk glanced out the windshield. They'd reached the old aluminum gate. The guy riding shotgun hopped out of the van. He took a long look around, then crept to the gate and opened it.

"Maybe they sleep," the Middle-Eastern man said.

Kirk searched the horizon. He saw nothing but trees and yellow-green grass. He guessed the morning hour at seven at the latest, but time didn't mean a thing to Jake's crew. He shook his head. "These guys are serious dudes. A couple vans full of paramilitary types wearing masks … they would've stopped us by now. Hell, I'm half-surprised they haven't taken a potshot at us yet."

The shotgun rider stepped up into the van. They rolled through the gateway. The American interrogator said, "Maybe they're all dead already. Maybe we waited too long."

Kirk wiped sweat away from his forehead. He avoided eye contact with the American. He knew the asshole meant they should've tortured the location of the camp out of Kirk instead of letting him come around on his own.

The van curled around and parked next to a couple of pickup trucks. The side door slid open. The masked men disembarked, one of them at his back, prodding him with the barrel of a gun. He jumped into a patch of straw-like grass. He took in the barracks and the storage shed. He looked to the north, towards the firing range. He mumbled, "Weird." He knew some of Jake's crew lived out here. The place shouldn't be deserted. His captors fanned out and beat the bushes. They showed efficiency and experience, even though their blue jeans and long-sleeved shirts suggested they'd be more at home on riding lawnmowers. They didn't speak as they combed the camp. The Middle-Eastern man lurked a few feet away from Kirk, while his wrangler stayed behind Kirk. He assumed the man stood ready to gun him down if he made any funky moves.

Kirk lowered into a crouch. He sat in the tough grass. He rubbed the tape on his wrists. He lowered his head. They were already gone. She would've known that the longer they stayed here the better chance the cult would catch up to her. Jake would know places to go. So his betrayal didn't hurt her. He looked up as the men reassembled near the vans. Didn't hurt her, unless they were telling the truth.

He judged the treeline at about twenty yards away. Thick weeds and stunted, yet whip-like saplings choked the spaces between the enormous old-growth trunks. A million places to hide. Probably, a few feet in, the dense foliage would deflect gunfire. His hamstrings strained as he stretched out his legs. His stiff muscles would fail him. He needed to catch them napping. Then after he lost them, all he needed to do was find a phone and call Jake. Then he would find out the truth. He shut his eyes and scrutinized himself for any remaining wisp of that instant genius, of that insight. He inhaled, but he couldn't tell if he was imagining the faint whiff of spice. His search turned up only his memories of the euphoria, of the ecstasy. He opened his eyes. At least, at the very least, once she understood what he'd been through …

"Where are they?" The Middle-Eastern man said.

Kirk peered into the trees. "Give me a little time to narrow it down. Right off the bat I can think of a couple of dozen places they might have gone." He studied the grass between his legs. He couldn't let them catch him measuring, calculating. He had to get ready without them noticing.

A shadow hovered over him. He squinted up at the American interrogator, who planted his hands on his hips and said, "You're lying. They were never here."

Kirk shook his head. "I swear, I sent her here. Maybe, maybe she didn't make it, or maybe she figured you'd get it out of me, and they went somewhere else."

"Or," the Middle-Eastern man said, while looming behind Kirk, "you are still in the power of it, and it is using you to misdirect us."

"Take us on a wild goose chase," The American said.

"If that is true," the Middle-Eastern man said, "then torture is futile."

"We won't know till we try," the American said.

The American stalked toward the van. No doubt to get that damned drill. Kirk bared his teeth, but stopped as soon as he sensed them chattering. He flexed his fingers. He said, "I'm telling the truth."

"I imagine that Miss Bosh is reaching the end of her usefulness," the Middle-Eastern man said.

Kirk twisted and glowered at him. "So the mummy would kill her? That doesn't make any sense, when it could just leave her behind."

"By now," the Middle-Eastern man said, his brow furrowing over his dark eyes, "she has been exposed, unprotected, past the point of no return. She would follow it to the ends of the earth, crawling when her legs failed her, until she dies."

Running footsteps pounded the dirt. A masked man, huffing, said, "We found something." The man wheeled and hustled toward the gun range. Another man yanked Kirk up to his feet and herded him along with the others. Kirk used the jogging pace to work the kinks out of his leg muscles. They passed the storage shed. He cut his eyes from the range, the sawhorses and the targets, toward the forest. A lone cult member aimed his assault rifle at the treeline.

The cult member in the lead halted and raised his palm towards the pack. "Shhh, listen."

Everybody stopped dead in their tracks. Once Kirk caught his breath, the *tink* made him flinch. A few beats sludged by, then *tink*. The reverberations disgusted Kirk. The gunmen closed in on the source of the sound. From the tangled foliage, Kirk discerned the strange clutch of weeds, the tassels intertwined at the top, the stalks leaning inwards, creating a sort of mini-teepee formation.

The men surrounded the clutch. They trained their weapons on the next nerve-grinding *tink*. Kirk had to force himself not to imagine the instruments making that grating sound. One of the men swept back the weeds. A man sat Indian-style in the center of the clutch. The sunlight gleamed off of the fork as he stabbed the utensil into his bloodied forehead. The resultant *tink* made Kirk cringe.

The American snapped his fingers and commanded, "Bring him!"

On either side men seized Kirk by the upper arms and escorted him towards the man. Blood trickled down from his punctured forehead. One of the outside tines of the fork bent inward.

"Do you recognize him?" The American said.

Kirk blinked. The chubby man wore a green and brown camouflage uniform. Kirk shook his head.

The American faced the bloody man. "Where'd they go?"

"They went for a boat ride." The man gave them a wide, toothy smile. He stabbed the fork into his forehead. The violent *thonk* made them all shrink back.

The Middle-Easterner stepped abreast of Kirk. "Do you believe us now?"

Kirk gagged, almost swallowing his tongue. He coughed, then said, "I know where they went. They went to Jake's island."

"Do you know where it is?" The American said.

Kirk nodded. His legs went numb. The men held him up and dragged him back towards the vans. He found his footing and caught up to their stride. He had fucked up. He'd stalled too long. He willed the image of her sitting somewhere in the gloom, stabbing herself in the forehead with a fork, out of her mind. *No.* That poor bastard, forking himself in the forehead, he must've suffered the same devastation, the same loss, that Kirk had, and the madness was simply the aftermath.

The American, somewhere behind Kirk, said, "Put him out of his misery."

The single gunshot echoed as they muscled Kirk into the van.

Chapter Eleven

The mummy opened the cabin door. Lesley had grown used to seeing the big green rubber boots and hip-waders, which she supposed the mummy found in the men's lockers. *Smart*, protecting his bandages from the sea water and salty air. The mummy had added a creased and faded black leather jacket over a black hoody. *Cliff's*. The massive size of the new gear left no doubt. The hood hid most of the mummy's head. The disguise, along with the seismic collision that had occurred a few moments ago, suggested that they'd run aground where the mummy wished to disembark.

She rose and followed him through the mess and up the stairwell. She couldn't wait to get off the boat. Two days since that horrible night, she'd only left the cabin to scrounge food in the mess. The mummy came and went on mysterious errands. He seemed to return to the cabin in order to reenter a restorative, catatonic state. Even so, as he laid on the bunk for hours, she felt the promise of things to come.

She raised her eyes to the heavy gray sky. The gloom merged with the sea at the horizon. The low, unbroken clouds seemed ready to burst, ready to unleash a biblical downpour. She stared at the island. She knew the hanged man, and the rest of the dead littered the deck. She didn't need to see the carnage.

The island emerged as a lighter gray than the sea and the sky. Slimy rocks rose from the lapping waves. Long sloughs of stone-studded mud curved a few feet above sea level. She supposed that high tide submerged this smudge of land.

She placed her palm on her stomach. She had no idea why the mummy chose this place, but she had faith. Finally it was just going to be the two of them. She searched for a way off the boat.

"Fuck!"

The shout spun Lesley. Her whirl slowed, the sudden motion dizzying her. She couldn't close her eyes. Her vision tilted sideways. The oppressive grayness muted the mangled face of the hanged man. Shreds of skin flapped from his chin. Fractured facial bones spiked out from his cheeks. Before she could look away, she imagined seabirds perched on his shoulders, their beaks rending his face.

She narrowed her eyes as her vision listed back to its horizontal aspect. The expected scattering of corpses eluded her. She allowed her eyelids to relax to a more open position. No dead men littered the decks. The creaking of the cord would not let her ignore the one remaining body. She drifted toward the other side of the deck. She found the source of the shout.

A man grabbed a large crank arm, and lunged into his work. Each screeching revolution lowered a ramp towards the shallows beside the boat. She didn't recognize him, but his dirty pants, thick sweater, and ragged watchcap identified him as one of Cliff's sailors. Another seamen stepped into view along the railing. The lowering ramp appeared to anger him. Violent jerks contorted his lips. Lesley assumed that running aground, the boat's weird angle, and the difficulty in disembarking in rocky, shallow waters prompted the pair's muttered curses.

The one cranking the winch threw his head back, and, his entire body trembling, sending a quaver through his howl, said, "I did it!" He dropped his head and hissed, "I did it I did it!" Still trembling, the man regripped the crank, and first a notch at a time, then picking up speed, he resumed his labor.

Lesley crossed her arms over her chest. She balled her fingers into hard fists. The deadly battle, the seaman's strange admission, she deduced that these cold hard facts implied that the mummy could not gain full control over the men.

She unlocked her right fist and brought her cupped palm to her mouth. *Maybe* … she whipped her hand away from her lips. She retucked her fist under her elbow against her chest. That bloody night … *unintentional*. He tried to fend off the avarice of the different factions. Even Jake had exhibited signs of greed. If there had been any other way … the effort must have drained him. He would not waste precious energy trying to manipulate her. Not when she already knew what was in store, what was at stake. The deaths were horrible, but losing him to one of those factions ….
unthinkable. Fatigue accumulated around her eye sockets. The salty air made her blink. He must have only been able to keep this pair alive. They were proof that he didn't intend the slaughter, or he would've let them die too.

A prolonged scrape sounded from floor level behind the door to the bridge. Higher up, several short bursts of pneumatic whirring preceded wooden thunks against the floor. Lesley nodded. The pilot had taken great pains to barricade himself inside the bridge. No wonder Jake hadn't been able to budge the door.

Pain pulsed up from her fist. She released her vice grip on her pained fingers and shook them out. She whispered to herself, "Don't be him, don't be him." The door opened, and *he* stepped over the threshold. She groaned.

Gizmo's face reeled toward her. His eyelids flattened to slits. He raised a knee and leaned into a slow, ungainly step toward her. His bony chest heaved under his baggy gray tee shirt. He passed his hand down his forehead, as if to flip down the visor of his helmet, which he'd discarded somewhere along the way. She interpreted the gesture as evidence that he resisted the mummy's attempts to stymie his advance.

Gizmo took another awkward, stork-like lurch toward her. She backed up and brushed the mummy, who stood with his back to them. Gizmo stooped and snapped up a nasty meat hook. The air seemed to solidify in front of him as he high-stepped toward them, his boot rising, then hovering, before its slow descent to the deck.

A tremor snaked through her knees. Her eyes darted back and forth, seeking a weapon on the deck. The mummy's power could only delay Gizmo's revenge.

Tink.

The metal-on-bone impact sickened her. Gizmo, a runnel of blood trickling from the middle of his forehead toward his eyebrows, swung the hook from his side in a semicircle into his skull.

Tink.

Another runnel of blood sprang from the new puncture in his forehead. He let the hook fall from his fingers. The bloodied tool clattered onto the deck. He swiveled toward the middle of the boat. He marched, his gait normalizing. Out of the corner of his mouth, he spat, "You, bitch!" He joined the men working on the ramp.

The men staggered down to the water. The mummy started toward the ramp. The slight bend of his knees gave his motion a doddering affect. Lesley hooked her head and neck underneath the mummy's arm and took as much of his weight as she could. He felt lighter. She detected the barest hint of rot. She exhaled, then took a big whiff, but she only smelled spice. She redirected her entire concentration on negotiating the rusted slats of the ramp.

Gizmo and the others waded toward the shore. She and the mummy touched down in the gray water, which rose to her thighs, much deeper than she expected. The lapping water threatened to dislodge her from her rocky footing. When her boot missed stones, mud tried to suck her boot off of her foot. She looked ahead at the unforgiving slab of gray land. She set her jaw. The mummy must have a good reason to come here.

Chapter Twelve

The American interrogator glared at Kirk. "You better be right this time."

Kirk's stomach acids churned. He squeezed the boat's railing and said, "I'm pretty sure." As the spotlight swept from the shoals to the rocky mud that formed the beach, he started to doubt himself. "Can you have them aim the lights higher?"

The American barked, "Higher!" The spotlight lit up the trees.

Kirk leaned over the railing. He dropped his head and closed his eyes. Finally, after half a dozen tries, he'd found Jake's island. They'd made no secret that he'd reached their last nerve. The American had accused him of stalling. He'd explained that he hadn't really paid attention the times Jake had piloted him out to the island, and those trips always occurred during daylight hours, and under the influence. He hadn't realized how many little islands crowded the coast.

Kirk raised his head. He surveyed the trees. Maybe this wasn't the place. He glanced sidelong at the American, whose bandana mask did very, very little to hide his impatience. Kirk knew the asshole had brought the drill onboard. Kirk peered into the dark trees. Jake and his men would have haled them by now, unless they were hiding in the trees, guns ready to mow them down as soon as they set foot on the island.

Kirk straightened to his full height. If he could find some way to identify himself to Jake without alerting his captors, and maybe drift away from them, then he could make his escape. As they circled the island and cruised toward the dock, Kirk saw no sign of Jake and his men, but he grew certain that this was Jake's island.

"No boat," the American said.

"Knowing Jake," Kirk said, "he had one of his guys pilot it away after dropping them off."

They dropped anchor along the wooden dock. Masked gunmen swarmed down the ramp. The American herded Kirk behind the gunmen. Kirk trotted, expecting the command to ring out from the trees, to stop and identify themselves. The American stayed on

Kirk's heels. The squad of masked men tromped over the dock and fanned out over the island. Kirk stepped onto the muddy land and tried to look innocent while hunting for his chance to bolt. One of the gunmen called out, "Got something."

A few men congregated at the shoreline. The relaxed position of their assault rifles suggested no immediate danger.

The American prodded the small of Kirk's back. He said, "Let's take a look." The American goaded Kirk to the cluster of masked men, who parted. A septic stench made Kirk flinch. He raked his forearm across his watery eyes while muttering, "Christ." For a moment, he couldn't process the bloated mass lying half in and half out of the water. He seized on the camouflage pattern and recognized the misshapen uniform. One of the masked men toed the corpse over onto its backside. The dead man's eyelids sunk down into his obviously empty eye sockets.

"You know him?" The American said.

Kirk nodded. The familiar mustache made him think of the name Grady, or Brady, something like that. The dead man had been one of Gizmo's good buddies. A wave of nausea forced Kirk to look away from the corpse.

A pulse of electricity dissolved his nausea. He dropped ass-first into the mud. He sank a good inch into the muck. That musical insight flared on the peripheral of his consciousness, but eluded his grasp. The mummy was near. He twisted over onto all fours and whipped his head back and forth. Mud sludged over hands. He sniffed, he opened his mouth and tasted the air. The mummy was near, Lesley was near. He hunched his back and groaned. They would know that he betrayed them. Unless she was already dead. He shook his head. *No.* He would sense that.

Masked men jogged up to the American. One said, "Found a cabin. Looks like nobody's been here in a while. Haven't found a trace of anybody."

The American planted his hands of his hips. "Goddamnit."

Kirk felt the heat of the American's glower. He refused to make eye contact. He sought that thread to the mummy. The connection loomed just outside his perception, as if he listened hard enough and in the right direction … as if tuning an old-timey radio just right … he exhaled. He twisted around and sat in the mud. *Just out of reach.*

The Middle-Eastern man's sinuous whispers in the American's ear distracted Kirk. He didn't need to hear the words to understand their discussion. He had led them to a dead end. They no longer had any use for him. They only had to decide whether or not to kill him. He refocused on that thread, he imagined the mummy on a boat moving away from them, and if the distance became too great, he would lose the thread altogether.

"Bring him to the body," the Middle-Eastern man said. "It is worth a try."

A pair of masked men hooked him under the armpits and hoisted him to his feet. He elbowed his way out of their hands and said, "Hey, I can walk!"

The American pointed at the corpse. "Touch it."

"What?"

The American crossed his arms over his chest. He gave the Middle-Eastern man a long look and said, "It's not gonna work."

"What's not gonna work?" Kirk said.

The Middle-Eastern man faced Kirk. "Are you sensing anything? Touch the carcass anywhere, skin to skin, and that feeling should be strengthened, if …" He raised a slender eyebrow.

Kirk knelt beside the corpse and touched the back of the poor bastard's hand. The slimy, cold texture made Kirk's skin crawl. Then the connection flared. So bright his entire nervous system jerked. He resisted the headrush and mumbled, "I feel it."

The American groused, "He'd say anything to save his skin. He's done nothing but stall."

"What choice do we have?" The Middle-Eastern man said.

Kirk rose above the dizzies. He got a handle on the crazy burst of energy. He aimed his eyes at the American. "I'm your only shot." Even though the feeling leveled out, he knew he could maintain the connection. He *knew* it. He could lead them to the mummy. Now was the time to make sure that their deal was ironclad. He broke contact with the corpse. The beacon did not weaken.

"We can stop wasting time," the American said. "We can admit defeat, and prepare for what's coming."

Kirk shifted his eyes toward the Middle-Eastern man. "I can take you to them."

The American looked down his nose at Kirk. "Relax. It'd be a waste of time to kill you. But we aren't gonna ferry your ass home, either. You can find your own way off the island."

Kirk pictured himself stranded. The connection would eventually fade away. "No," he said. "I can feel them … when I close my eyes I can see it, almost like radar."

"Just as the others …" the Middle-Eastern man said.

"What others?" Kirk said. Neither man bothered to glance at Kirk, much less answer him. Kirk did the math. "What happened to the others?" Again, neither men seemed to notice him. If they had others that could pinpoint the mummy's location, then they wouldn't have bothered with him. So that meant they died. And the cult wouldn't have killed them, because they would have been useful to the cult. So that meant either enemies of the cult murdered them, or … "What happened to the others?"

The Middle-Eastern man clucked his tongue, then said, "Prolonged separation, once a connection has been established, has proved fatal. In every case."

Kirk stood up. He took a step back from the corpse. He said, "How?"

"How do you feel?" The Middle-Eastern man said.

"I feel like shit." Kirk inventoried himself, but with the pain of his raw wrists, and the muscle and bone aches of his long imprisonment, he couldn't tell. "I feel bad. But you guys tied me up and didn't give me water for who knows how the fuck long." Kirk's burst of anger surprised even himself.

"In any case," the Middle-Eastern man said, "you now have a vested interest in reestablishing close proximity. That is the only cure."

Kirk's anger withered. They could be lying to him. This could all be a show for his benefit, to trick him. He winced. "Will it happen to Lesley too?"

The Middle-Eastern man shrugged his thin shoulders. "You witnessed that unfortunate man in that camp. His exposure must have been minimal. If it has not already abandoned her to die, if she is not already dead, your only chance to help Mrs. Bosh is to lead us to it."

He gagged. He felt like he kept swallowing his tongue, even though he ran it over the backs of his teeth. He still couldn't pinpoint anything bad happening to him. Even if he'd been … *metaphysically* poisoned, it still didn't mean the mummy was evil. But he couldn't bet her life on it. He lifted his chin. *That* should do it. He did the math again. They meant to destroy the mummy, believing they would save the world. So what would happen to Lesley and himself after the mummy was destroyed? *Fuck.* But if they were telling the truth, she could be dying right now, or the mummy could end the world. He stared at the mud. He couldn't win. *Fuck it.* Let it all burn. He was never gonna get her anyways. Fever heat circulated through his forehead. He was never gonna be a great musician.

"You're right," the American said. "We should try. But we should prepare for failure."

"Mr. Taylor," the Middle-Eastern man said. "Kirk. If you do nothing, if you mislead us … you cannot succeed. But if you lead us, you have a chance, you must realize this, no matter how little you trust us."

Kirk wilted in on himself. He couldn't argue with that, even if he could muster the strength. But he could fuck them over whenever he chose, if he so chose. "Okay. I can show you the way."

Chapter Thirteen

Gizmo, with a screech, jerked away from the muddy soil. He cradled his wounded hand between his thighs. He glared at the mummy. *Tore a fingernail off.* Lesley winced. Gizmo's agony haunted her own index nail. He lurched toward the mummy. He froze. Trembling, his rage contorting his face, he stepped into a slow pivot. He whined, "Why don't she have'ta dig?"

Lesley's knuckles whitened around the unlit flashlight. Gizmo managed to halt his turn. A shaky gurgle escaped his lips. The other men stopped digging. Gizmo growled as he resumed his turn. He sprang towards the muddy wall, mashing face-first into the soil, his arms spread wide. He grunted, and with an exaggerated arc, slammed his injured hand into the dirt. He howled, but he kept digging. The other two men joined him.

The pain in Lesley's fingers rose to a visceral level. She relaxed her grip on the flashlight. The mummy had regained control. The men clawed at the dirt, which crumbled down to their feet. Mud smeared each man beyond his elbows, and streaked their torn clothing and lacerated faces. The men had resisted the descent into this crevasse. All their resistance had accomplished was more cuts and bruises.

A sliver of gray light above her marked the cleft, which she would've missed on the surface of the island's muddy, rock-strewn mass. The mummy led them straight to the cleft. They'd all scraped their way down to this pocket. She couldn't help thinking about high tide, the sea water cascading down and filling this shaft.

The mummy showed no anxiety. The rubber boots, the hip waders, the faded and creased black leather jacket, and the sweatshirt underneath, with the hood pulled over his head, made him seem like just another man. He stood deeper in the pocket, between her and the men, who couldn't see that precious sliver of open air while they dug in the gloom.

A stony grind accompanied a rain of dirt and mud. Several rectangular slabs slid upward and downward, revealing two rows, each slab grating at different speeds and times. The men back-peddled away from the commotion. The filing-cabinet sized slabs vanished into their housings. The last drizzle of dirt sifted to the floor of the pocket. Lesley blinked. If they wanted, the five of them could walk abreast through the passage.

Light. Lesley snapped out of it and flicked on the flashlight. The mummy and the men advanced into the passage. Each man's gait matched the stiff-legged walk of the mummy. Lesley followed behind them.

She raked the beam across the spacious ovaloid chamber. The walls, the ceiling, and the floor glistened, wet but not muddy. Still, the floor sucked at her boots. She lit up the far end, where a door-sized passage led into the blacker darkness. The mummy marched the men toward the passage. The men merged into single file. Their gaits continued to ape the mummy's, except for their heads, which twitched back and forth, up and down, while they rasped a nearly stream-of-conscious series of confessions. Their various admissions of animal tortures, of spying on female relatives in states of undress, of petty theft, of date rape, of self-aggrandizing lies, and of so much more, wearied her. She wished the mummy would leave them in the pocket of the crevasse.

She studied the chamber as she trailed behind them. Some kind of springy rock made up the floor. Perhaps the moisture softened the texture of the stone, she didn't know, that sort of thing was not her field. She sought indications of culture, but not a single scrawl adorned the walls. Perhaps the absence of aboriginal artwork implied a much more advanced civilization than one would expect.

She frowned. The mummy's knowledge of this secret place, located in the northern Pacific, blew up all previous theories of the mummy's true origins. This discovery suggested a lost civilization. Not simply a culture that mummified its dead, but a people that discovered a mummification process that in reality was suspended animation, a technology that contemporary cutting-edge science could only laughingly approach in the form of cryogenics. This technology must have seemed like black magic to adjacent peoples, who, perhaps, banded together to destroy their more advanced neighbors. Or, *or*, maybe Atlantis was really located in the Pacific!

Lesley took a deep breath. *Get a hold of yourself.* She slowed her pace as she reached the passage. They were going somewhere, where, she had no doubt, everything would be revealed. Perhaps the mummy needed something to communicate the hidden knowledge that she knew he possessed. Mind control, suspended animation, even the mechanics involved in the barrier to this chamber, these were just the tip of the iceberg.

She stepped through the doorway. The downgrade of the passage forced her to lean back a little in order to maintain her balance. The footing remained secure. The moist ground adhered to her soles, almost to the point where she suspected an audible pop every time she worked her foot free. The increase in air pressure weighed on her eardrums.

Gizmo snarled. He pressed his palms into the ceiling. "This is so gross!" he said. "I can't take this! I'm claustrophobic!"

Lesley shined the light over the men. The tunnel continued to narrow. She held her arms inside the scope of her body, not wanting to graze the wet walls.

"I ... will ... kill you!" One of the men said. His decelerated to a near stop. He accelerated, while quaking, until he returned to the mummy's pace. The mummy's exertion seemed to allow Gizmo and the other man a moment of respite, during which they slowed too. Their visible efforts to free themselves calmed as they returned to walking speed as well.

Lesley caught herself squeezing the flashlight again. She wanted to tell them to submit, things would go easier for them if they did, but their constant striving for subversions implied that they were beyond the reach of reason. She could only assume that they still needed the trio, that their presence was worth the mummy's tremendous pains to control them.

She smiled. *That's it!* The differences between herself and the unwilling men proved the mummy wasn't influencing her. Because she knew the rewards, the mummy did not need to coerce her. But if he was, she'd feel it, she'd resist being guided into this scary as hell tunnel, on some primal level, and the mummy would find it necessary to move her along, and she would feel it!

Her smile vanished, her countenance grew solemn. She wasn't better than them, that wasn't it. She simply had the training and possessed the qualities that allowed her to comprehend what was at stake here. Gizmo and his fellows, if they had the chance, would sell the mummy to the highest bidder and be done with it. That difference didn't make her better. She nodded. It made her *luckier*.

Her shoulder brushed the wall. A substance clung to her jacket before puckering back against wall. Her slender frame permitted her to center herself in the passage, but the ever-narrowing chute forced the men and the mummy to angle and to duck their way along. She couldn't reconcile the pliable substance with the tunnel's apparent stability. Obviously, the substance coated packed earth or stone. She circled back, time and again, to waterproofing, the only answer that made any sense to her. As to why the mummy's people would construct this underground hideaway ... *secrets, dark secrets* ... she flinched. *No.* That was just some latent, primal instinct, prompted to rear its superstitious head on account of this strange passage. Fear of the dark, fear of the unknown, and yes, even Gizmo's claustrophobia ... *yes.* Wasn't even coming from her. They were all connected now, and some of Gizmo's, and the other men's, irrational fears were bleeding over to her through the mummy. She nodded. And that's how she knew, because the mummy would block such psychic residue, and, and ... shut off her primal instincts. That's how she knew the mummy wasn't manipulating her.

Relief washed over her, and she realized the relief emanated from the men when she stepped into the bulge in the passageway. The chamber's ceiling rose to twice Gizmo's height. The walls spaced wide enough for all of them to stand comfortably apart. Her flashlight's beam found no change in matter, the sticky coating surrounding them. But her nose detected a faint char underneath the mummy's cumin and clove scent. She surmised a fire pit, to ward off the underground chill, lied nearby.

"Aaaaarp!"

Lesley aimed the flashlight towards the abrupt scream. A floor-to-ceiling cyclone enveloped one of the men and increased its velocity, rending his clothing and flesh, then blood, organs, and bones, into bits, which clouded the cyclone but remained within the ghostly wobble of the upside-down cone. With wet smacks, the bits glommed together, forming larger masses, which sank lower within the cyclone. These darker masses pressed and folded into one another. The cyclone died. A single mass splatted onto the ground. Roughly the size of two side-by-side loaves of the bread, the mass's darkish color blended in with the ground, the walls, and the ceiling.

The floor gave a slight pulse. The mass seemed to resist a downward conveyance, ripples in its texture imparting a scrabbling

aspect. Lesley shuddered. The sticky substance coating …
everything. A billion bugs seemed to crawl over every inch of her
skin. Her stomach contracted. The mass lost a few more millimeters
on its slow melt downward.

Calm yourself. You are in no danger. Her nausea dissipated.
So did the creepy-crawly sensation. The mummy's doing.

She swept the beam towards him. He'd placed a hand on the
shoulders of both Gizmo and the other sailor. Seizures shook
through their bodies, their eyes rolled up in their heads, their spines
locked out straight. The mummy released both men. Gizmo
remained in a convulsive state. The other man took an arduous step
forward. He muttered, "No." The mummy matched his step. They
took a more supple step in unison. And another, and the man
screamed, "No!"

The cyclone whirred into life. The mummy continued,
passing through the inverted cone unscathed. He stopped on the
other side. Lesley averted her eyes until the *splat.*

Gizmo started forward. His torso listed backwards, but his
legs kept moving forward. He sputtered, "No, no no no no no!"

Come. That single word echoed inside her skull. Gizmo
would trigger the cyclone, and she could pass through it unharmed.
Or she could remain on the other side and her part in what was to
about to happen would be over.

Lesley followed Gizmo. The cyclone shrouded him. She
hesitated. The mummy wouldn't need to trick her if he wanted her to
suffer the same fate. She dashed into the cyclone, meaning to rush
through to the other side.

Pressure closed in on her, slowing her progress. Gizmo's
hatred, pure and blazing, encircled her. She gritted her teeth and
strained every muscle into the effort of pushing forward. His desire
to take her with him crushed her lower. An image flickered into her
mind, an endless row of empty wooden chairs perched atop columns
of mismatched stones. The image distracted her from Gizmo's fury
long enough for her to surge out of the cyclone. She landed on all
fours at the mummy's feet.

He extended a hand and helped her up. The cyclone had
already finished its work. The mummy turned and walked into the
passage. She rose. She took a step and her boot squished on the
ground. She aimed the flashlight at her feet. She'd stepped on one of

the masses. She skittered away from the dented blob, which continued its fight against the slow downward thrum of the passage. She wondered if, standing still, the passage would carry her too.

She hurried to catch up to the mummy, who moved faster now that he didn't have to control three men. They came to a fork in the tunnel. As she suspected, the pulse carried the masses down one fork, while the tunnel the mummy selected exhibited no signs of motion.

She shook her head. The mummy had to sacrifice the men in order to gain her and him safe passage. They were murderers anyways. She frowned. Were they? She recalled Gizmo's cunning glances, his not so subtle attempts to take possession of the mummy, and his inner being, through which she had passed. Rotten to the core. And a necessary sacrifice. Her frown deepened.

Chapter Fourteen

A ragged cough exploded out of Kirk's mouth. The guard inched further away, towards the cabin's opposite wall. Kirk would bet anything that under that bandana mask a look of disgust warped the guard's face, as if Kirk's cough was contagious. Kirk shrugged. Maybe it was catching, maybe the mummy had poisoned him. Maybe poison had caused all that madness surrounding the mummy's history. Or maybe his illness was psychosomatic, maybe his worry about being sick was making him sick. *Sick, sick, sick.* Kirk laid his palm across his mouth. He eyed the guard, who exhibited no reaction. He must've thought it, not said it out loud.

He slouched against the molded plastic seat. The Middle-Eastern man said that the mummy was the cure. He closed his eyes and waited for the radar-like image to flutter into focus. He couldn't really explain the sensation to them, he just knew when they were headed in the right direction, and he knew when the boat veered off course. And recently, the intensity had increased, to the point where he felt a lump in his guts. The lump kept growing harder and heavier. He couldn't help thinking 'tumor.' Before, when he opened his eyes, that cancerous impression faded almost down to nothing. But now the lump kept getting bigger. The American had accused him of faking it, had pulled him aside and warned him that if he was bullshitting then he was dead meat. If the asshole had any idea, he'd shut his damned mouth. The lump had swelled so much that Kirk feared it would tear through his guts. The discomfort was driving him up the wall.

He grabbed the edge of his seat, in preparation for levering himself to his feet, but he stayed down. He didn't want to spook the guard. But he was dying to go topside. If his captors were telling the truth, then they should spot Lesley and mummy any minute now.

He released the edge of the seat and clasped his hands in his lap. If they were telling the truth, then Lesley was in danger. He leaned forward. He needed to warn her. He collided with the same mental brick wall. If he was poisoned, then she was poisoned too. They were both doomed, unless they could somehow escape the cult, with the mummy, and stay with it forever. He could see no other solution. But they would have to go through paramilitary types prepared to deal with the mummy, and the mummy appeared to have some do-or-die purpose of its own. He and Lesley … either they were gonna end up dead, or, at the best, left behind. Lesley would blame him for her separation from the mummy. She would hate him.

Kirk slumped back into his seat. Maybe he should just give up, like the American wanted to do, but instead of regrouping and preparing for the worst, he should try to provoke them into murdering him. Maybe rip the mask off the American's face, that should do it. If they were telling the truth, the whole goddamned world was about to end anyways. He'd die a no-talent hack, unloved, unmissed, so fuck it all. Hell, he probably wouldn't have to provoke them. The cult probably planned on killing him once he'd led them to the mummy anyways. They probably only kept up the masks to maintain the illusion that he had a way out of this mess.

He sat up straight. If they were telling the truth … but if they weren't … the Middle-Eastern man claimed that the corpse that they'd found meant that the mummy had discarded all of Jake's militia buddies, except those few it found necessary to serve its world-destroying purposes. He claimed that was the mummy's method of operation. They wanted Kirk to suspect that the mummy had killed Lesley too. *Lies.* He'd been there, when the mummy first awakened. He'd shared a connection with the mummy, and with Lesley. There'd been nothing but good … no, *great* things in store. Just a few minutes' contact with the mummy had removed that mental block that Kirk had always, *always*, known was there, was preventing him from realizing his full potential. Sure, there was the corpse, and that poor bastard back at the camp. He closed his lips. The cult had murdered that poor bastard. Not the mummy. The truth was nobody knew what happened to the dead guy. The feeling in his guts … they could've put something in his food and water to make that happen. He maintained a poker face. It was too late to lead them astray. Lesley and the mummy were near. The only thing he could do was to play along, and hope for a chance to get the three of them out of this, and if he couldn't do that, he'd sacrifice himself so that they could get away.

Kirk felt no surprise when masked men entered the cabin and announced that they'd spotted a lifeboat. Kirk sprang to his feet. The rock in his stomach seemed to throb. *Probably nerves.* His hackles rose as they marched him topside. He tried to calm himself, he told himself to be ready for anything.

A couple dozen men, bandana masks drawn up to their eyes, had assembled on the deck. Kirk followed their collective gaze. In the gray expanse of sky and sea, he spotted the orange octagonal life raft. The raft drifted too far away for him to see its inhabitants.

A man lowered a pair of binoculars. "One occupant. Not it."

Kirk winced. *No, no, no ... they ... they were gonna be pissed*, they were gonna think that he misled them on purpose. He parted his lips to smile. His cheek muscles felt tight, like he hadn't smiled in years. Had to be Lesley. His attempt at a smile flattened. She might be sick, maybe even ...

He stepped toward the rail. The American pointed at him and said, "Sit his ass down and if he makes a move, shoot him."

Men seized Kirk and spun him away from the rail. They forced him to sit on the deck with his back to the distant raft. They trained their assault rifles on him. He drew his knees up to his chest and hugged his kneecaps to himself. He closed his eyes. They could stop him from seeing, but they couldn't stop him from feeling.

Men barked orders and affirmations. Cable spun on reels. Something splashed in the waters. Among the hubbub, somebody said, "It's a man."

Kirk rubbed his palms over his face. It was good that it wasn't her. That meant she wasn't stabbing a fork into her forehead. That meant she wasn't slowly dying.

The American called out, "Bring him here!"

Masked men hauled Kirk to his feet. He elbowed his way free of their grip, hissing, "I can walk!" They guided him back towards the railing. Once through the first rank of paramilitary assholes, he whispered, "Jake."

His friend's back was propped against the railing. Jake sat with his legs extended before him. Somebody had wrapped a bulky blue jacket around his torso, and draped another such jacket over his legs, but Jake's bedraggled tee-shirt and khaki shorts peeked out from the gaps. Despite Jake's obvious hardships, his stubbly bald head and bristly red moustache made Kirk smile a little.

Jake's brown eyes sharpened as he gaped at Kirk. He said, "Hey."

Jake tried to kneel beside his friend, but his keepers held him back and forced him to stand upright. "I'm sorry," he said. "I didn't know."

Jake clutched a proffered canteen and took a deep drink. He lowered the canteen. He nodded. "I–"

"Where are they?" The American said.

Kirk ground his teeth. Fatigue softened Jake's stare, which did not waver from Kirk. Jake said, "It was like … it was like riding in the passenger seat of a car … but the car was driving itself … you know what I mean?"

The plea in Jake's eyes caused an excruciating shift of the mass in Kirk's guts. Kirk had to lie, he owed Jake too much to deny him any measure of solace. He nodded.

"I watched myself choke a man to death," Jake said. "And I couldn't stop myself."

Kirk shook his head. "It wasn't–"

"Where are they?" The American said.

"I'm sorry," Jake said. "I couldn't protect her … but give me another chance. I can help, you know I can, I got weapons, secure bases, food and water, you know this, everything we'll need for after."

The Middle-Eastern man pitched his voice gentle, saying, "After what, my friend?"

Jake looked at the Middle-Eastern man. "I wanna go home." He faced Kirk, but a cloudiness came over his eyes. "Please, just let me go home."

Jake lunged at Kirk. He vised his hands around Kirk's throat. Kirk sputtered. Men tried to peel Jake's hands away from Kirk. Blackness smoked into the periphery of Kirk's vision. One snap after another sounded. Kirk realized they had to resort to breaking Jake's fingers. Jake's grip released, his fingernails raking Kirk's gullet, and Kirk gasped for air. Some men dragged Kirk away and laid him on the deck. Kirk flinched at a gunshot. A heavy splash followed. Kirk closed his eyes and muttered, "Oh fuck. Oh fuck oh fuck oh fuck."

Kirk drew hitching breaths. He sensed somebody near him. He looked up at the masked Middle-Eastern man, who crouched beside him. The Middle-Easterner said, "It left your friend as a decoy, as a time bomb. It anticipated the possibility that you might become a bloodhound."

Kirk felt his stomach, searching for any protrusions over that mass. He found nothing. "He'd still be alive if it wasn't for me."

"You are fortunate it did not force you take your own life when it abandoned you in the museum."

Kirk bit his tongue. He understood that it had needed him alive in order to slow down the cult.

The Middle-Easterner said, "Now that your friend has passed, you should be able to locate a new destination."

Kirk closed his eyes. He could, just like before. He nodded.

The Middle-Easterner patted him on the shoulder. "The sooner we find them, the better chance she has to survive. Allow me to convince my colleagues that pressing on is the best course."

A burst of coughs rattled Kirk. He sat up. He pulled his legs up and rested his forehead on his knees. *Damn, damn, damn.* He raised his head and scanned the men, but nobody paid him any mind. He must've thought it, not said it. He put his head back down on his knees. The Middle-Eastern man had to convince the American and all the other men who wanted to give up. They must realize too, that the mummy could've planted dozens of decoys in their path. Including Lesley herself. They would scurry all over the Pacific, hell, all over the world, while the mummy took its sweet time doing whatever the fuck it planned to do. Nausea contracted Kirk's stomach and compressed that mass in his guts. He grimaced. Maybe it was better to give up. He didn't want to catch up to Lesley, if the mummy was gonna make her try to kill him.

Chapter Fifteen

Lesley ducked under a cluster of glistening prongs, which jiggled above her. She eased her boot up from the gunk underfoot, mindful of the moment when the clingy substance allowed her sole to pop free, in case her momentum propelled her head into the grossness an inch over her skull.

On the other side of the oozy overhang, her flashlight's beam lit up an oblong cavity. She followed the mummy into the cavity. The muck coating the floor thinned, granting better footing. She relaxed a smidge. At least she didn't have to worry about the slime sucking the too-big boots off of her feet. In spots, the floor solidified from the springy, trampoline-like give of the tunnel. She swept the beam across the far end of the chamber, which appeared to have no other exit.

She aimed the beam at the floor and spotted a jagged fissure in the sticky film. She approached the naked ground and tested it with her toe. The slight compression suggested some sort of porous rock. She whispered, "Definitely not manmade."

She trained the light on the mummy, who used his booted feet to scrape the sticky stuff away from a large clearing in the goop. Maybe the subtance was manmade. She raised her left hand and brushed her lips with her fingertips. *This was it*! This place must be the key to revealing the promised knowledge to her. The hidden door, the device that protected the tunnel, the bizarre substances, all of it screamed lost culture. A culture perhaps not the equal of hers in all respects, but certainly a culture that had made great leaps that contemporary science could only dream of.

The mummy stopped scuffing at the gunk and planted both feet shoulder-width apart, facing the far wall. A dim brownish light flickered, then steadied. The world seemed to spin, until Lesley realized that the walls *were* moving, albeit at a glacial pace.

She scrunched her eyelids shut, then took another look. Currents emerged, weaving over and under each other, and individual portions broke off and skimmed this way and that. Her leg took an involuntary swing and her boot came down on naked floor. Before she could frown, the sentient agony swamped her senses.

Somewhere among that turbulence, she felt a reciprocal recognition. *Gizmo*. A numbness replaced her awareness of that swirling agony, but before the reverberations died out, she captured the gist that some technology similar to that which had preserved the mummy would preserve Gizmo's self, intact but trapped in that transmuted form, both fuel and component of this antediluvian mechanism … perhaps forever.

She tried to move her foot but her leg, her body, wouldn't budge. She managed a warped cry. No passageway, sudden loss of motor control, archaic machinery, she couldn't shove away the inescapable conclusion that the mummy was about to sacrifice her in order to pass another barrier. Her cry waned and died in a whispered "No."

Her eyelids lowered. She strove to keep them up, to seek a way out, but their descent did not slow, and she entered total darkness. Sparks sprayed against the black backdrop. At first the color of lightning, the sparks gathered and flashed through the spectrum, reds, blues, yellows, greens, and then dazzling through layered combinations. The collective sparks stabilized into larger shapes, which pivoted, revolved, gyroscoped, while others remained still, but all gained depth, contorting into the third dimension, and even the tranquil shapes exhibited motion, quivering, distorting at their edges. She swayed, free to move, but an epiphany followed her release, that she shared this experience with the mummy, that the shapes formed patterns, a message, a language, that the mummy deciphered with ease. *This was it*!

She curled her left hand into a fist and thwacked her thigh. She shouldn't have doubted. He had promised her. He wanted what she wanted. Horrible things had happened. *A test*. And she had almost failed. She gave a slight shake of her head. No, he hadn't tested her. He would know that she harbored doubts, that the horrors on the boat, and the conversion of Gizmo and his cohorts, would shake her faith. He was a product of an aeon when lesser but more numerous peoples committed genocide against his culture. What seemed like abject cruelty to her was hard necessity to him, for survival, for a last chance to share lost knowledge, which, perhaps, would save humanity from itself. She smiled, she beamed. This was the beginning of … *everything*.

She focused on the symbolic play against her blackened interior. The sophistication of the language proved the sophistication of his lost culture. Here and there, she caught curves and lines, combinations, that hinted at basic shapes in the ancient alphabets with which she possessed familiarity. A dash of Greek, a Phoenician stroke, an Egyptian glyph, and the hypothesis burst into her head, that she was bearing witness to progenitor of written language. The inspiration to less-developed peoples, who imitated the snatches they were able to comprehend, their own reproductions crude, rudimentary facsimiles of this primordial marvel.

She raised her chin and craned her neck. Her smiled widened. She felt certain that the tingling in her head signaled the creation of new neural pathways, that exposure to this miracle was lighting up the dark regions of her brain. Soon she would grasp the basics, then the nuances. The concepts that required such intricacy would shatter the boundaries between science and sorcery. The mummy's very existence implied that even death could be overcome.

She observed the symbolic spectacle against her inner darkness. She expected that the mummy would impart the key to translating the text at any moment. She noticed a low whine escaping her lips. She tamped down that expression of frustration. *Patience.* Perhaps the mummy was reading how to bequeath her the necessary ability at this very moment.

She clamped her jaw and screwed up her forehead. She bore down on the problem. He hadn't granted her the easy way because she must already possess the aptitude. Or he had already bestowed the tools, and the process of discovery would lead her to proficiency, perhaps mastery, of the convoluted language. If one person could read it, so could another. She focused on stationary attributes, attributes that triggered anything close to recognition. Every thread slipped out of her grasp. The changes, mutations, subtle or radical, came too fast, too garbled for her to discern any patterns. All she could do was to assume that every, *every,* minute variation imparted information.

She expelled a grunting breath. Perhaps she wasn't up to the task. She certainly couldn't digest the totality. Her sob surprised her, and revealed how far down she'd already spiraled. The mummy was trying to share his knowledge with her, his sharing of the experience confirmed his effort. She simply was not intelligent enough to understand.

An electric surge inspired Lesley up from her despair. The surge gave her goosebumps. The confusing array of shifting symbols vanished from her mind's eye. And she *knew*. This cavity was not their final destination. He had intended it to be, but the object he required to make her understand … *everything*, had been stolen. But the thieves did not know that a beacon had been secreted within the object.

Or …

She opened her eyes and glared at the back of the mummy's hooded head. Maybe she was wrong. Maybe this was just the next step in his plan. Maybe he knew that the object would not be here, but access to the homing signal would be. And if she was wrong, maybe she'd been wrong all along. An image shimmered into her mind, the mummy sticking the vague object into a cartoon Acme-style machine, which chuffed on, and then an interstellar view of a cartoon Earth, its elementary grin transforming into a surprised expression right before it exploded into smithereens.

Her teeth chattered, the clatter of her molars dispelling the childish vision. She scoffed. Only her imagination running wild. Her worst fears cartoonish in their immature stupidity. The object was part of a tool that would permit her to understand. She nodded. Shame sludged up from deep within her guts. She knew he could see straight into her heart of hearts. He knew her doubts. He knew her fecklessness, her lack of faith. She staggered off of the naked flooring and into the sticky gunk. She raised her hands to her face, her right fist still gripping the flashlight. Her skin felt cool to the touch.

She dropped her hands from her face. The mummy was already walking back the way they came. The motion of the walls and the ceiling had ceased. The lights were dimming. The mummy reached the exit. The lights winked off. She pointed the flashlight at the mummy. She fell in behind him. They still had miles and miles to go.

Chapter Sixteen

A blitz of jagged coughs tore up Kirk's throat. The violent fit provoked a trickle within his left nostril. Through a series of quiet sniffles and a pinch that he tried to pass off as scratching his nose, he managed to stop the trickle before the blood leaked out of his nose. He glanced from one side of the deck to the other. The nighttime darkness shadowed their faces, but none of the cultists seemed to notice his struggle to hide his latest symptom.

He bent toward his knees while crossing his arms over his chest. He clamped his hands on his biceps and stifled a groan. He pictured what he must look like to the others. He sat up straight on the plastic housing. He rested his palms on his kneecaps. He had no idea what the plastic rectangular protuberance underneath him contained, but the perch gave a good view of the deck and the dark sea.

He stared towards the horizon. His vision blurred. He could chalk up the cough to being held in that goddamned trailer without water for so long, or just getting sick because of the way they'd treated him. He rubbed his stomach. If he pressed hard enough, he felt the hard mass in his guts. Hard to think of anything but instant tumor. Hard to stop thinking that exposure to the mummy had caused a pre-existing condition to accelerate, or maybe made the clash of a few free radicals stick together, a clot that otherwise would've broken apart in the natural course of things. He sniffled. Throw in the nosebleed, and he could no longer deny the obvious. But the only way to know for sure was to see if rejoining the mummy alleviated his symptoms.

He sucked his lower lip between his teeth. He bit down until the pain made him stop short of breaking the skin. Lesley could be suffering the same symptoms, or even worse, with her longer exposure … *if* the mummy had abandoned her too, like the Middle-Eastern man kept insinuating.

He caught himself drumming a frenetic beat on his kneecap with his fingertips. He clasped his hands together. He'd been up and down it, back and forth, and he couldn't find a way through to the other side. Lesley was gonna hate him. He narrowed his eyes, but he wouldn't allow himself a full wince. Unless he led the cult astray. *And*, exposure to the mummy was not poisonous. *And*, the cult was lying about the mummy's true nature. If all that fell just right, then he would protect Lesley. Of course he would remain a no-talent hack. *And*, the cult would surely murder him after they discovered his treachery.

The barest hint of a snarl distorted the corner of his mouth. *So what*? He was living in dreamland if he thought Lesley was ever gonna love a loser like him. And his asshole captors were right, he really didn't love her, if he wasn't willing to sacrifice what he wanted for her best interests. And he didn't really want to live anymore anyways, a mere shadow of what he could've been, realizing just how much of a hack he'd always been. And if his asshole captors happened to be telling the truth, then that gift of musical insight was just a trick, so that the mummy could seduce and use him. And then Lesley was a goner too, as soon as she was no longer useful to the mummy. So fuck it, let it all burn down to ashes.

His long, hot exhalation irritated his throat. He managed to suppress another round of coughs. In the search for a shred of truth, he kept coming back to the same question. Whose actions were more evil? The cult tried to steal the mummy. They'd imprisoned him and threatened to use a power drill on his fingers. Not only did they coerce him into betraying the woman he loved, they also tried to convince him that his love wasn't real. On the other hand, the mummy … *possessed* … people in order to escape the cult. He touched his Adam's apple. The tenderness persisted where Jake had tried to throttle him. A sheen of moisture shimmered his vision, but no tears slipped beyond the rims of his eyelids.

A bitter laugh dried his eyes. He deserved this, every single bit of it. He'd already betrayed Lesley. He could dress it up any way he wanted, but he'd betrayed her. Probably the mummy's gift of musical genius was just a trick, because that would make things as worst as possible, no matter what he decided to do. *Fuck, fuck, fuck*!

He gnawed on his lower lip. He might've sworn out loud. From under his brow he eyed the nearest cult member, who paid him no mind. Seeing them without their bandana masks still weirded him out. Some of them looked like genuine paramilitary-badasses, but some of them, like this one, looked as soft as cubicle workers. He couldn't decide if losing the masks meant that they planned to kill him, or that they'd come to consider him an accomplice. And probably their bare faces represented a veiled threat, meant to prey on his mind, to keep him on the straight and narrow, and that implied that they had at least debated whether he might try to mislead them. The American certainly didn't try to hide his suspicions. The asshole believed that their mission had failed, and that the apocalypse countdown had already begun. The American had proved his commitment by unmasking first. Since civilization was about to end, he didn't have to worry about facing any legal consequences for his actions. The American champed at the bit for End Times. Probably wanted Kirk to mislead them.

Kirk tried to muster up a sarcastic laugh, but his wheezy production sounded fake to his own ears. He might lead them straight to the mummy by accident. His ability to track the mummy had started to cut out a while ago, and the blind spots kept stretching longer. Right now he had no idea if they were on the right course.

"Yo," somebody called out, "got something!"

Kirk's knees creaked as he rose to his feet. The spotlight exposed a fishing boat drifting on the black horizon. He hurried to the railing and peered towards the boat. He couldn't see a soul.

The American herded Kirk over the gangplank and onto the fishing boat. The American had ignored Kirk's questions about the advance team's search. As he stepped onto the fishing boat, his soles squished dents into the deck's rotting wood. A fishy stench welled up and invaded his nostrils. While trying to snort this the stench out of his nose, he scanned the boat for any sign of Lesley, or the mummy, but only cult members occupied the topside.

The American escorted him to the Middle-Eastern man, whose long, thin lips and slender nose looked almost exactly like Kirk imagined. Kirk looked away from that man's penetrating brown eyes. The sloppy spooling of a nearby roll of cable left the coils in disarray. Long peels of white paint flapped from the outer walls of the bridge. A hatch door laid ajar in its frame on the deck. Kirk figured this neglected boat teetered on the edge of qualifying for derelict status.

"Do you know him?" the Middle-Eastern man said.

Kirk tracked the angle of the Middle-Easter man's upraised arm and bony index finger. A corpse sagged against the cables lashing it to the top end of the mast. Right below the corpse, one of the cultists clung to the mast with one hand and worked a tarp down from the corpse's torso with the other. From below, a flashlight beam lit up the dead man's bluish face and lolling dark tongue. Kirk spotted the noose encircling the dead man's neck.

Violent contractions seized every muscle in Kirk's body. *The noose his own traitorous fingers weaved dangled around his neck.* Hands caught Kirk and laid him on the sodden wood. Shouts swirled into nonsense. The Middle-Eastern man's triangular face hovered over him. *His hand gripped the hold above and the upward yank tweaked his low back. He tried to stop his progress up the mast. His effort seemed to jettison him further away from retaking his motor controls. He couldn't even scream.*

"Relax Kirk," the Middle-Eastern man said. Somebody else said, "He's gonna tear meat right off the bone if he don't quit!"

Kirk's vision clouded. He tried to focus on the concerned brown eyes. *He stared down at the deck. He let go. The short drop snapped his neck. Command returned to him even as numbness seeped into his limbs. He gurgled.*

Kirk gurgled. His spine bowed, raising his backside off the deck. He collapsed. He tried to speak. He produced a croak.

"Bring him water," the Middle-Eastern man said. "Now!" He lowered his voice into a soothing pitch, saying, "What did you see?"

Kirk foretasted a fresh round of contractions. He said, "No," right before the seizure hit. *Everybody's out to get me. He squeezed the handle of his favorite hunting knife. His AK jounced against his back. Use the knife for stealth purposes. Use the gun after they get wise.*

Kirk flopped back to the deck. His entire musculature throbbed. The seizure rebounded. He sucked in a deep breath. His body stiffened, but he coped this time. He kept the contractions from reaching the max intensity. The men kneeling around him persisted. But a different point of view superimposed over their faces, and the starless void above. The sea rushed up at him through the faces. A rib bone wrenched the knife's hilt out of his grip. His finger froze on the trigger. The Middle-Eastern man grabbed his elbow and eased his arm back to the deck. He watched two men tumble over the railing and splash into the black sea. Blood spattered across his neck and chest. He latched onto the Middle-Eastern man's stare and pulled his consciousness upward. He sputtered water out of his mouth. "That's enough," the Middle-Eastern man said. The water bottle whisked away from his lips. A brutal spasm launched his torso upwards. Hands lowered him to the deck.

He watched a man wriggle into a nook between the bridge's outer wall and a pile of refuse.

A chattering of tics rattled his resolve.

He strained to see into the sooty haze. He watched a pilgrim scuttle behind a jumble of trunks. The buoyant floor jounced his bare soles. He noticed the faint dampness of the material squishing up between his toes. A vague form darted after the pilgrim. A super-soprano scream yodeled a tritone twice. In the ensuing rest, the screechy interval echoed in his ears, and charting its overtone series he pinpointed its tonic fourteen, no, fifteen Hertz below true C-sub-seven.

He blinked. The Middle-Eastern man's face swam on his periphery. Tiny pinpricks of starlight dotted the deep darkness above him. Hands pressed his body flat to the slimy deck. He relaxed his cramping muscles. He focused his consciousness on the near blackness above, connecting the dots, creating imaginary staffs and clefs, notes and motifs. He wove motifs into songs. He prepared to weave those songs into greater pieces, intuiting how all of it could fit together into one whole, but the dots, lines, and curves faded. He arched his back and stretched his hands toward the sky.

They forced him back down to the deck. Somebody said, "Make sure he don't swallow his tongue!" They wedged his jaw open. Gizmo, Cliff, the petty criminals who crewed this dilapidated boat, they would rape, they would murder her. *Him. Lesley.* He lunged for the residue, then realized he didn't need to, as her fears flooded into him and blotted out everything else. A snatch of a hulking man going overboard preceded the recession of her fears. The mummy's influence steadied, *had* steadied her. *No, is* still steadying her. He felt her through the mummy, who acted as a sort of psychic router. Her fear persisted, but at manageable levels. He picked up strands of doubt, too, hushed but discordant notes within the rich angel-chorus of her faith in the mummy. Their proximity manifested itself in this sudden revelation of her innermost heart, and in the mummy's deafening white-noise hiss. *And,* the resurgence of that unlimited musical potential. He grazed the possibilities, he only needed to make contact with the mummy again, and he would recapture the whole thing.

He stared into the starless night sky. He only needed to betray Lesley. A hot runnel ran out of his nose towards his upper lip. He smeared the blood with the back of his hand. He laid his hand over that mass in his stomach. He couldn't be certain, but the mass seemed smaller and softer. He shifted his eyes to the Middle-Eastern man and said, "There's no more decoys."

The American's puggish face leaned into view over the Middle-Eastern man's shoulder. "He could go all psycho on us any second now," he said. "Look at what just happened!"

The Middle-Eastern man performed a slight upward tilt of his head. The American straightened out of Kirk's field of vision. The Middle-Eastern man's brown eyes lasered in on Kirk. "Will you take us to them?"

Kirk nodded.

"We will bind you, for both your and our protection."

"I would if I were you."

The Middle-Eastern man stood up and gestured to the others. As they sat him up and tied his hands behind his back, Kirk surveyed the dark sea while enduring the fresh aggravation to his scourged wrists. He understood how little prompting, how little energy, the mummy had needed to send certain men leaping over the railing.

Chapter Seventeen

Heat blasted Lesley. At the core of that broiling gust, Gizmo's familiar hatred, his living hatred, his perhaps eternal hatred, stabbed at her soul. She raised her hands in front of her face while ripping her sole free of the gunky floor and jamming that foot into a backward step. The heat evaporated. His hate lingered through a slow disintegration. She lowered her hands. She redirected the flashlight's beam to the way ahead. She didn't need Gizmo's psychic residue to recognize this place, beyond the fork in the tunnel.

She aimed the flashlight at the ground. The brownish muck revealed no trace of a triggering mechanism. The muck just maintained that almost imperceptible downward oozing. The light revealed nothing suspicious on the walls and the ceiling, just the same salve-like muck, the same downward undulation.

The tunnel's customary coolness reasserted itself. She shivered. She swiped away the sweat persisting on her upper lip. She itched to glance at the mummy, whose slowing gait had conceded the lead to her a while ago. The math made sense, a solution simpler than that old logic teaser of how to get a fox, a chicken, and a sack of corn across a river. Gizmo and his pal to get her and the mummy through the trap, and then she gets the mummy back through the trap. Her consciousness would spend eternity sludging with Gizmo's, reduced to a sentient dollop of goop.

The mummy loomed behind her. She balled her free hand into a stiff fist and, with the other, choked the flashlight so hard its housing crackled. All he had to do in order to allay her anxiety was to go first. *Unless this was a test!* She loosened her fist and her grip on the flashlight. She knew he saw straight into her deepest, darkest heart. He had to know that she harbored doubts. He possessed the power to take over her motor controls. Or maybe emotional manipulation was less taxing than physical puppetry. Proving to him that she could overcome her doubts about his true mission, proving that she still believed she would receive the promised rewards, and that she still believed that the global benefits would far outweigh all the necessary atrocities … she slumped. Inculcating the desire to prove her worthiness required the least exertion of all, a timeworn tactic of every charlatan in history. The carrot waved in front of her nose only to be whisked away right as she leapt off the cliff.

She shook out her tense shoulders and arms. *Screw it.* She yanked her foot free, her boots sinking into the muck during her hesitation. Her forward stride resulted in a squelch, but nothing else. A snarl rumbled across her lips. She stomped into her next step.

She barked up a relieved laugh. She knew she had passed the danger, but she needed another half-dozen steps to work the wobbles out of her legs. She'd passed the test. She wondered how many times she'd argued with her religious friends about the difference between faith and knowledge, that the concept of faith demanded doubt. Real, honest-to-goodness, maybe tipping-the-scales doubt. She nodded. This sort of thing shouldn't be easy. A truly evil being would make things seem easy.

His footfalls grew more labored, more sluggish. She hung back and let him catch up to her. She put his arm around her neck and helped him walk. She knew the effort had cost him. Now the slight upgrade and the sticky ground sapped his remaining strength.

She hoisted him out of his slouch. Energy buzzed through her veins. She would carry him if she had to, all the way to the mysterious object. She gazed into the darkness in front of them. *Soon* … soon the darkness should lighten as they reached the end of the tunnel.

The darkness endured as the climb steepened. When the flashlight lit up a dead end, the closed slabs didn't surprise her at all. The mummy gestured towards the adjacent wall. The flashlight's beam struck a lever at about head height. Lesley left the mummy standing before the doorway. She grasped the wet, rough stone lever, and pulled the rod downward. The lever resisted, then a distant twang preceded its precipitous drop. The door slabs didn't move.

She hung her head. Calmness flowed over her despair. She knew the mummy was soothing her. She faced him. He staggered to the slabs. His bandaged hands stuck out of the too-long sleeves of the faded black leather jacket. He jabbed his swaddled fingers into the cracks between the slabs and strained to raise one of the stone rectangles. She stuck the flashlight into the gooey floor so that the angle provided him light. She rushed beside him and threw her back into the task.

She pushed down on the lower slab. Her hand slipped to its neighbor, and she felt the stone shift. She switched to the loose slab and put all her weight into pushing it down into its housing. A nighttime drizzle breezed through the widened cracks. Between the two of them, they created enough of a crooked gap for the mummy to scrape through the space. She turned to retrieve the flashlight. One hand still on the lowered slab, she felt the stone rising. She wriggled through the gap before the slabs ground shut. She belly-flopped onto the mud.

She crawled next to the mummy, who'd made his way to the far end of the crevasse before stopping. She rolled onto her back. The chilling rain pattered on her face. She pulled herself into a sitting position. The mummy didn't move. She tried to flip him onto his back, but she couldn't budge him. The dark sky obscured the top of the crevasse. She closed her eyes. The current connecting the two of them seemed to ebb to an all-time low. She had to get him out of here. Then back to the boat. Then she had to figure out how to pilot the boat.

She rasped in a breath. The rain plastered her hair to her head. She punched her thigh with the side of her fist. She growled, "One step at a time." She dragged the mummy onto his back. She hauled him up so that his back leaned against the crevasse wall. Completing this one small chore drained her. She plopped down next to him in the mud, and laid her forehead on his shoulder. She whispered, "Please." Maybe this was it, maybe he'd spent himself getting them this far.

Brightness flooded the crevasse, blinding her. She shaded her eyes and squinted. Dark figures rimmed the top of the crevasse. She threw herself over the mummy and screamed, "No!"

Chapter Eighteen

Kirk made sure of his footing in the mud. He leaned over the edge of the fissure. The squad's high-wattage flashlights illuminated individual raindrops of the steady drizzle. Kirk leaned further while tucking his bound wrists against his chest for balance. The muddy floor of the chasm extended cave-like beyond the reach of the light. His hackles stood on end. *Their* energy baked out of the pit and beckoned him downward. "They were here," he said.

The American scoffed. "Meaning that they're not here now."

Kirk straightened away from the fissure's edge. He dropped his hands from his chest and relaxed his shoulders in order to quell the heated rush of anger. He knew the American and his faction wanted, at best, to abandon him on this desolate pile of rocky muck that passed for an island. Best not to provoke the asshole.

The Middle-Eastern man murmured, "You are certain?"

"I need to go down there," Kirk said.

Kirk raised his bound hands to shield his face from the light rain. He watched the last member of the team rappel into the fissure. The man's efficiency, as he lowered himself while seated in a rope harness, caused Kirk to reassess the presumed softness of some of these babyfaced dudes. However, the Middle-Easterner declined to make the descent. No such luck with the American, whose breath Kirk felt against the back of his neck.

Kirk stamped away from the asshole. He shouldered past the half-dozen men already in the pit. He stepped up onto the drier mud under the rock, which loomed a few feet over his head. He stopped in front of the far wall of the compact recess. He raised his crisscrossed, bandaged wrists and placed his palms against the flat stone. His scalp tingled. "It's confused," he said. "But it gets stronger here."

He coughed. The cough's shallowness relieved him. The others had started from the bottom of his lungs and ripped up his throat. He sniffled. No scent of blood. He rubbed his stomach. He felt the hard mass protruding just under his skin. *Fuck, fuck, fuck*!

He glanced over his shoulder. They stared at him, as blank as ever. Nobody gave any indication that his dismay had escaped his lips. He chewed his tongue. These lapses, when he couldn't tell if he'd spoken or just thought something, distressed him as much as the tumorous mass. He used to make jokes about spiraling into madness. Shit didn't seem funny anymore.

A finger-print sized oval sparkled on the wall. Kirk scrunched his eyes shut, then opened them. The shoulder-high sparkle brightened. Kirk pointed at the oval. "Anybody else seeing this?"

"See what?" The American said.

Kirk pressed the ball of his thumb against the oval. A rumble warned Kirk to back up, and he bumped into the American as an upper row of five panels, in a disharmonious sequence, grated into slots, and a lower row, also out of sync, dropped into their slots. Within the darkness, a flashlight, fixed at an angle in the ground, back-lit a lone lingering lower panel. The cave mouth and its single obstructing panel reminded Kirk of a Jack-O-:Lantern's sinister grin. "They went inside," he said.

"No shit." The American said.

Kirk's first step inside the cave produced a gummy squelch. He halted. In an awestruck tone, one of the American's men said, "The Devouring Cave." His proclamation hushed the rest of them. Kirk pivoted. Under a few inches of goop, the ground supported his weight.

Another man aimed his flashlight at Kirk's face and said, "You shouldn't go in there."

Kirk shielded his eyes. He addressed the American, saying, "What is it?"

The American snorted. "Some mumbo-jumbo obviously based on a kernel of truth." He pointed at Kirk while twisting toward the others. "He's already inside and nothing's happened to him. Anybody who wants to be a pussy can wait out here."

The American strode into the cave. He raked his flashlight's powerful beam up and down and across the cave. The greasy goop coated everything, except a stone lever on the wall to Kirk's left. Kirk jabbed his bound hands toward the downshifted lever. "It's broken," he said. He faced the tunnel leading into darkness. His scalp's tingling intensified into a full-on buzzing. "If I go down there, I can find out where they went."

The American stooped and snatched the dying flashlight out of the goop. He switched it off and pitched it underhand, but with a bit of assholish English on the toss, to one of his men, all of whom remained outside the cave. "Who's coming?" He said.

Four men accepted the American's challenge. Kirk noted that each exhibited different levels of confidence, from bravado to outright fear. The American snickered at the men who loitered outside. "You ladies make sure those doors don't shut!" He extended his arm while glowering at Kirk. "Lead the way."

Kirk took a deep breath. He headed for the tunnel. Their flashlights lit the way. Their steps joined his to create a jumble of percolating pops as their soles squished into then tugged free from the suckling goop.

The effort of pulling his boots out of the goop after each footfall caused a faint lactic-acid burn in his calves. He discovered that picking up the pace lessened the hold the goop got on his feet. Still, he didn't dare go too fast. His bound wrists reduced his balance, and he couldn't help imagining a fall into the crap and getting stuck like a bug on flypaper. His fear slowed his pace further in case he tilted one way or the other and splatted into the walls, which the goop coated too, as well as the ceiling. He supposed the others harbored the same disgust since they'd formed a single file, even though the downward-canting tunnel's span allowed them to march in pairs.

He explored the dampened echoes of their collective tread until he remembered the awestricken tone of one of the American's lackeys. He cleared his throat, choked down a cough, and said, "Why'd he call this the Devouring Cave?"

The American huffed a curt sigh. "You really don't know anything about this shit, do you?"

Kirk shrugged. "I know the story about the Rewrapped Mummy."

The American blasted a breath that made his lips flap against each other. "This thing's been creepin' around since our ancestors lived in caves like this ... well, maybe not caves like *this*, but you get my meaning."

Kirk nodded. He hadn't seen any living thing at all in this cave, no bats, not even a bug.

"The thing is," the American said, "Nobody knows much for sure, but that never stopped anybody from filling in the blanks with all kinds of crazy-ass shit."

Kirk nodded again. Sounded reasonable to him. "How'd a skeptic like you fall in with these true believers?" He heard the other four grumble under the noisy suction of their footfalls. He chided himself to rein in his barbs. The four dudes that decided to come along for the fun and games had to be part of the American's faction, part of the group that wanted to call off the search and go hunker in their underground bunkers. Hell, the American's willingness to pursue this lead surprised the shit out of Kirk.

"You've seen what it can do," the American said. "I believe in Evolution. With all my heart, soul, and most importantly, my mind."

Kirk frowned. He detected the lilt of a practiced argument, one that the American had perfected over the years, probably over beers with his confidants, and while killing time in the shower. Every point buffed and honed.

"Variation, selection, reproduction," the American said. "To think we homo sapiens were the only species variation is just goddamned arrogant." The American let his point hang for a moment, then said, "It is one of those weird mutations. Like us in a lot of ways, but its brain chemistry is different, more sophisticated. Hence, its ability to control the minds and bodies of others."

Hence. Kirk ran his tongue around the inside of his mouth. He yearned to say something like 'using the ninety percent of its brain that we don't,' but he'd never heard the American ramble so much, and he didn't want to interrupt. He sensed that throwing off the man's rhythm might make him realize that he was exposing his innermost self, might make him clam up. Kirk supposed the American's followers already knew this about the man, and that was why they were all ears. This man was deeper than your average paramilitary redneck.

"Its existence and its powers are not in question," the American said. "But all the myths that have grown up around it … it's like the division in Islam. Sunni, Shiite, that sort of thing. For every crazy notion that's taken hold around it, there's a bunch of whackjobs bowing around some fucked-up shrine."

The urge to stick it to him frothed up in Kirk again, but he swallowed his sarcasm along with the crack, 'But you guys are *soooo* different.'

"The Devouring Cave is akin to Scylla and Charybdis," the American said.

Kirk gave no sign that he had any fucking clue what the American was talking about. He noted that the walls of the cave had begun to narrow.

"Or," the American mused, "like Jonah and the Whale. I've spent most of my adult life investigating these legends. I've been a part of sects that believed some of the most insane nonsense I've ever heard in my life. Not a one of the crazier legends turned out to be true. But, that's all part of its game. Its playing chess while all these other sects are playing checkers."

Kirk glanced over his shoulder at the American. "But you believe that it means to usher in the Apocalypse."

"I don't profess to see the whole picture," the American said. "But I do know that everywhere it has gone, death has followed. In some cases mass deaths, genocide, that sort of thing. My best guess is that it has discovered the means somehow. Maybe some rich fuck funded a lab that developed a virus, or maybe some rogue government or terrorist organization has developed nuclear weapons, something like that, and now, after all these years of hibernation, it is on the move. It means to destroy us. My best guess is that it needs to eradicate us before it can repopulate the Earth with its own species. Or maybe its doing it purely out of hate, or evil. But it means to do something very, very bad."

A roiling headrush stopped Kirk in a widened portion of the cave. "Wait. Something happened here." He closed his eyes. Somebody cleared his throat. Somebody else shifted, creating a soft suckle in the goop. As if the volume dial started at zero and rolled to full blast, a swirl of wails and screams assaulted Kirk's eardrums. Lesley's terror silenced the anguished throng. Her blind faith in the mummy still shined through her terror. The blend staggered him, screeched at him that his next step meant death, followed by eternal damnation, his voice added to the howling mass of the endlessly tormented.

Somebody brushed past him and engaged the trap. Kirk, his eyes still closed, felt the snare shredding the man body and soul. An impulse nudged Kirk forward. He flinched. The impulse swelled. Kirk grasped that this impulse was the residue from the mummy's demand that Lesley pass through the Cuisinarting of some poor wretch's entire being. Kirk darted through the whirlwind. The edge of his trailing heel snagged. The miniature dust-devil spun him so that he faced the others. He stumbled backwards, and the dust devil disintegrated. He planted that lagging foot into the goop. The wedge missing from his heel caused him to teeter. He rocked onto the balls of his feet and back into the center of his balance.

A blob of goop oozed between his feet. He cringed. Now he understood what he was standing in, what surrounded him on all sides. The sound of diminishing stamps focused him on the others. The American and two of his men aimed their guns at him. The other guy must've decided to split. Standing still, Kirk noticed a glacial current in the goop. In the silence he heard the whispers, the differences in motion. The goop was not of a whole piece, but rather thousands of discrete blobs, some wriggling over others, but all seeping down the tunnel. He held his bound hands in front of himself. "I didn't know!"

"Bullshit!" The American said.

"I swear!" Kirk said. "I just knew, when it happened, to go through him." He didn't need to feel the magnetic force pulling at his psyche to know that answers awaited at the end of the tunnel. "I have to keep going, it's the only way to find out where they went."

The bill of the American's ballcap hid his puggish features, but Kirk sensed him mulling it over. The American lowered his gun. He tossed his flashlight to Kirk.

Kirk made the catch despite his bonds.

"We'll wait here," the American said. "But not forever. Get going."

Kirk hurried down the tunnel. The squelches of his feet blocked out all other sounds. He tried to stay attuned to warnings of further weird deathtraps. *Not a deathtrap. A transformer. A processor.* He nodded. This tunnel was really a corridor. This place was really a machine. Powered by the trapped consciousnesses. Forever.

At the fork, the right corridor might as well have been lit up in neon. The machine pumped most of the blobs down the other corridor. He imagined the sun burning out, the Earth cooling to a barren rock, and still this machine would run, performing its obscure functions, the trapped souls fueling the machine's engines until the end of time. His teeth chattered. His interpretation felt right. The chattering of his jaw spread to his entire body. He tried to forget that his every stomp landed on what was now the body of a trapped soul. He tried not to speculate whether or not they could feel the blows of his boots. He tried to relax out of his shivers, but his damp clothing and the corridor's chill combined to extend his shakes until they roughened into a fit of jagged coughs. He quickened his pace.

He saw double. The reverberations of Lesley's perceptions superimposed over his own. The residual energy emanating from the chamber gave him goosebumps. He stood where she had, on a slice of floor free of goop. His tremors vanished. He didn't bother surveying the chamber. Her point-of-view was more than sufficient. He felt her wonder, he felt her frustration, and her despair. He leapt from her to the mummy. He could only comprehend the iceberg's tip of the mummy's weariness. He shunted that futile quest to the side, and sought the truth about the mummy's supposed gift of musical genius. The mummy, the *thing* – the American's theory of a differently evolved being was right on the money – the mummy's obsession with total annihilation swamped Kirk. Every little move the mummy made served his obsession. Lesley's continued presence at his side served his pursuit of total annihilation. The mummy's tease of musical genius was equivalent to stoking Lesley's zealotry. Emptiness lied behind everything the mummy promised.

The seizure, which he didn't even know that he'd suffered, abated. He dropped to his knees in the shallow goop. He fell onto his bound hands, aggravating his rope burns. He moaned. His moan grew into a ravaging fit of coughs. Blood dripped from his nostrils onto a dry patch of floor. His coughs mollified into deep wheezes, each contraction of his abdominal muscles strained against that heavy mass in his guts.

He could just lay down. Die here. His misery would finally come to an end. His love for Lesley was stupid. He was a hack, always had been, always would be. The mummy had peered into his soul and used the carrot he couldn't resist. And Lesley was too far gone to open her eyes to the truth. She'd only hate him if he tried.

The blobs beside him shifted slug-like. He pushed himself back up to his knees. There was no end to misery in this place. He would become a literal cog in the machine, after this strange organic mechanism absorbed his flesh, blood, bones, and soul. *Fuck, fuck, fuck*!

He lurched up to his feet. The absence of an echo reassured him that he had not howled out loud. He slitted his eyes. Lesley would hate his guts, but he could still save her. He hissed through his bared teeth. His rage sharpened his focus, enough that he soaked in all the ambient psychic power he could hold. He could follow that thing to Hell and back now. He turned and ran back up the tunnel.

Chapter Nineteen

Lesley narrowed her eyes. Sitting cross-legged on the floor of the broad canoe, at the head of the mummy's laid-out and motionless body, she stared at the brown leather boots of the nearest 'islander,' who stood while plying a long oar. She knew they weren't legitimate headhunters, or whatever they were trying to sell. Snatches of white skin peeked out from under the woven grass and palm-leaf skirts and leggings, the wooden breastplates, and the outlandish tribal tattoos that snaked and whirled up and down their arms and hands.

Their ceremonial fright-masks reminded her of Gizmo's faction. Those exaggerated wooden visages had to house state-of-the-art jamming equipment. Tech that they believed would protect them against the mummy's psychic abilities. Also like Gizmo's wannabe-soldiers faction, these grim and taciturn men played at an image. But their Caucasian slips, as well as the assault rifles lurking beneath the tarps in each of the outrigger canoes that she'd had a chance to observe, spoiled the affect.

The choppy waters rocked the canoe, despite its stabilizing outrigger. She seized the sides of the wooden vessel. Once the canoe resettled, she exhaled, but she didn't let go. She didn't care about the size of the boats, or their authenticity. It was stupid to row across the ocean in these low-riding, low-tech crafts. They were gonna end up capsizing, and dumping the mummy. She reached her right hand to him, and rested her hand on the heavy links of the anachronistic chains wrapped around his torso. He hadn't moved since they'd escaped the cave. Still, they'd stripped him of the fishing-boat gear and wrapped chains around his body down to his ankles. They hadn't exhibited the same level of fear when it came to her, however, leaving her unshackled. She supposed she was lucky these silent men hadn't stranded her on the island.

The mummy's bandages caught the weak light of the graying rim of the eastern horizon. The creases seemed wider and darker. Lesley ran her fingertips between the windings. Moisture swelled the bandages. Grit roughened the interstices. The ocean air, the water, the mud, they all confused the issue of rot. She closed her eyes and sought that psychic connection. She strove to detect some sign that these strange men were a part of the mummy's plan. They'd needed help. It was like the mummy shut down, in order to recharge, allowing himself to fall into the hands of these Pacific-Islander imposters. She opened her eyes. She coughed. She wrapped her arms around herself. If only she'd been able to understand his language. She uncoiled and clutched the sides of the canoe. *Faith.* They were moving towards the object. They had to be.

Shouts startled her. The men in her canoe drew in their long-handled oars. They armed themselves with assault rifles. To the south, a boat hurtled towards them. The sleek V-shape of the boat quashed any attempt to define it as a fishing vessel. She couldn't doubt that they were coming for the mummy, who must have orchestrated this opportunity. She gathered herself into a crouch.

"We gotta do it now!"

She honed in on two men at the front end of the canoe. They faced one another. The wooden fright-mask muffled the voice on the one with his back to her as he yelled, "We're not over the trench yet!"

"We can't take the chance! This'll have to be deep enough!"

She rocketed to her feet. Somebody grabbed her from behind. His thick arms pinned hers to her sides. He lifted her off of her feet. The canoe lurched, the blade of its outrigger rose, then slapped the water. The man holding her backed away from the mummy as two other men positioned themselves at the mummy's head and feet. They hoisted the mummy. She screamed. They flung the mummy overboard.

She drove the flats of her feet into the shins of her assailant. She got in a solid shot that provoked a grunt out of him. His embrace loosened. She wrenched her elbow upward into the underside of his chin. The blow sent sparks of pain up to her shoulder joint. He released her. She vaulted into the ocean.

Her momentum dunked her under the surface of the brisk waters. She flailed to the sinking mummy. She grabbed his ankle and pulled herself hand over hand to his shoulders. She managed to arrest his descent, but she couldn't generate enough force to drag him upwards. The exertion sapped the oxygen in her lungs. She dove underneath him. She centered the crown of her head underneath his upper back. She kicked as hard as she could. The water pressure resisted her, but she made progress.

She held the mummy's head above the waves as she reached air. She took a giant breath. The staccato burst of automatic gunfire jarred her. The shooting escalated. She twisted for a look and ducked under the surface. She kicked back up, towing the sinking mummy up with her. Salt water stung her eyes. On the other side of the line of canoes, the attacking boat bleared. The corpses of a few islander-imposters bobbed in the waves on her side of the ocean. She maneuvered into a sidestroke, tugging the mummy along with her, making for the outrigger of the nearest canoe.

The water's chill penetrated her clothing. Her waterlogged boots and jacket taxed her muscles. Her pace slowed. Her head went under and she swallowed seawater. A desperate surge of energy propelled her to the surface. She sputtered. Her flailing arm sent up chaotic spouts of water. Blackness leeched into the periphery of her eyesight.

She growled, "*No!*" She willed herself back from the precipice. She locked her neck under his armpit. She forced her arm to perform regular strokes. She synched up her kicks with her sidestroke. The blackness receded. She kept his head above the water. Her saturated clothing taxed her legs. She used one foot, then the other, to shuck her boots. She worked the jacket off her arm, submerged, swam under the mummy while discarding the jacket, and popped up on his other side. Using her fresh left arm to stroke gave her a boost of energy. Her hand smacked against a wood rail. She clamped onto the outrigger.

Bursts of gunfire punctuated the frenzied clash of war whoops. She tried to rotate to see who had won, but the mummy submerged. His weight thwarted her heave. She pushed off the wooden rail and dove under him. Perpendicular to his sinking body, she thrust up into him. Her hands closed on the chains wrapped around him. She managed to shove him to the surface. She fluttered her hands over his body. She found the loose end of one the chains. She rolled his body once, releasing a loop of the chain. She held onto the end of the chain and thrashed to the surface.

She inhaled too fast and half a mouthful of brine choked her. She chopped her arm in the water. She gained a few more inches of elevation. She took in a hacking breath. The chain in her right hand jerked her under the surface. She dove below the mummy and loosened another loop of chain. She bulled him above the waterline.

She towed the mummy to the outrigger rail. She coiled the chain around the wood until she ran out of slack. She let go. Her jury-rigged lashing held the mummy upright. His shoulders rose above the waves. She clamped both hands onto the railing. She closed her eyes. A tremor traveled up through her body and chattered her teeth. Gunfire blurted here and there. She willed her shakes into stillness. She noted the numbness seeping into her skin. She had to get them out of the cold sea.

A solid mass smacked into her and tore her loose from her handholds. A fist thwacked her right between the eyes. Her vision doubled. She gurgled. She tilted her chin and spurted the water out of her mouth. She gasped. She flailed above the wavelets. One of islander imposters, still wearing his carved fright-mask, splashed towards the mummy.

He unwound the chains. His speed dazed her. Her mouth slipped beneath the surface. She sputtered. She screamed, "No!" She lunged towards them. The mummy sank out of sight. The imposter pushed off of the railing and surged towards her. She knew he meant to drown her, or at least hold her long enough for the mummy to sink beyond salvation.

A gunshot crackled. The forehead of the imposter's mask exploded. She managed to shut her eyes before the splinters, shards, and bits of soft tissue splattered against her face. She submerged. She opened her eyes. In the gray turbulence, she spotted the mummy drifting on a downward slant away from her.

She plunged after him. She caught up to the trailing end of the chain. She wrapped the links around her right fist. As she darted upward, the mummy whirled in place, unspooling another length of chain. Her wail released a swarm of bubbles. She dove to him. She wrapped one arm around him. She thrashed to the surface, beating back the impending blackout. She wheezed in a breath. A corpse nudged into her. She cringed from the dead body and wrenched the mummy's head above the water. Other bodies bobbed in the ocean. A circular life preserver struck the tip of her elbow. She tracked the preserver's line to the new boat.

Gunmen leaned over the railing. Some waved their assault rifles over their heads and cheered. Others scaled ladders down to the waves. She grabbed the foam donut. They hauled her and the mummy toward the ship. She scanned the outrigger canoes behind her. She didn't see any survivors, but plenty of corpses and free-floating masks littered the ocean between the now-unmanned canoes and the newcomers' vessel.

The craft's sleek and low shape created a sharp contrast to Cliff's poorly-maintained, barnacle-encrusted fishing boat. No mast, no rigging, no scattered barrels and bric-a-brac cluttered its topside. Just gunmen. Lots of gunmen. At first glance, their machineguns, bandoliers, and ragtag clothing reminded Lesley of newsreel footage of Somali pirates. But a second look revealed that tribal face-paint disguised most of the white faces goggling at her. She rested her forehead on the life preserver. Their chants, their howls, told her all she needed to know about their temperament. But the alternative was the mummy sinking to the bottom of the ocean, as well as drowning for her. With a groan, she raised her weary head. At least these new zealots seemed intent on saving the mummy.

The men on the scaling ladders fished her and the mummy out of the sea. Fatigue swept away the blip of anxiety as a man threw her over his shoulder, thus separating her from the mummy, who required two bearers to reach the boat's railing. She let herself go limp. She closed her eyes and sought their connection. She blocked out the man's shoulder pressing into her stomach, and the sway of her upside-down head. Distant, but there, she picked up the message to rest, to marshal her energy. She did her best to remain limp as other hands pulled her off the man's shoulder and over the railing. The howls and chants died out, sharp commands replacing the jubilation. Shivers coursed through her body. Somebody carried her inside a cabin. Other men wrapped her in a rough, but thick and warm blanket.

The drop from mutters to a general hush prompted her to open her eyes. Six men carried the mummy into the cabin, pallbearer-style. She struggled to see through crowd, which backed into a thick mass in order to make room for the procession. The men lowered the mummy into a lidless wooden casket. Lesley found an angle that allowed a view of the ornate carvings decorating the coffin, but men kept shifting into her sight line and preventing a precise indication of the pictograms. Still, like her previous captors, this sect also harbored pretensions of ancient traditions, they just stopped short of the costumes and props. Except for the war paint. The green and blue whorls, the red and black slashes, seemed more

Gaelic than islander to her, albeit with a post-modern, Scandinavian death-metal slant.

The hushed whispers fell into silence when a bald man entered the cabin. Lesley sat up straight. His blue nylon jacket and matching track pants swished with each stride. He shot a sharp glance at Lesley, his thick black eyebrows contrasting with his pale shaved skull. *He felt it too.* He shared her connection to the mummy. *No. Not shared.* Not any more than a guttering candle in a boundless abyss shared the illumination of a sun going supernova. She swept her gaze around the room. Her previous captors had secreted blocking mechanisms in their masks in order to protect themselves from the mummy's psychic abilities, but these men, they offered themselves. She understood that they bestowed great honor on the bald man for his rare induction.

The bald man leaned over the casket. He placed his palm on the mummy's chest. A beatific smile banished his solemn expression. He proclaimed, "He walked! The eon of Apollo is over, the eon of Dionysus has begun!"

Cheers erupted from the men, who flung their hands in the air, jumped up and down, slapped each other on the back, hugged, and jabbered. They danced, swirling into a moshpit-like mayhem. Several akimbo elbows jostled Lesley farther against the wall. She concentrated on their shaman. His mind, his desires, his schemes transmitted loud and clear to her, as did the cult's dogma. They were true blue, dyed in the wool Bacchantes, worshippers of wine, song, dance, and sex. And chaos. They believed the mummy was the god himself, hibernating until it was time to usher in pandemonium. But tucked underneath the sediment of pious trappings, the shaman's bloody ambitions glowed. Lesley knew he would lie about her importance to the mummy. He meant to manipulate the malleable devotees into tossing her overboard.

For less than a heartbeat, she trembled. Her eyelids descended to slits. A low growl escaped her gritted teeth. She launched herself away from the wall. She blasted through the capering zealots, losing the blanket in the melee. She threw herself over the casket. Her fingers locked around the bald man's neck. He batted at her shoulders and face. She centered the balls of her thumbs on his Adam's apple and crushed his throat. Her grip persisted through his backward topple, which pulled her over the casket and onto the floor on top him. She didn't let go until he stopped moving, until she extinguished his inner flame.

She reeled to her feet. The frenzied dancers had stopped. Her lips moved, her voice crackled to a harpy's shriek as the words clawed their way out of her mouth, "I am his true special! I am your true guide!"

She swooned. Hands caught her. Faraway, she heard their uproar, which ignited the resuming of their exultation. She fought to remain conscious, but she felt herself slipping away. She knew they had ceremonies. She knew that they would replace her with one of their own, if they could. But the mummy had chosen her. He had *inhabited* her. She wouldn't have been able to murder the shaman on her own. She moaned. Her awareness shrank to a pinprick in the blackness. She was an academic, not a high priestess of debauched religion. She shuddered, then slid all the way into the darkness.

Chapter Twenty

Kirk's stomp jarred his flashlight into winking out again. He rattled its lens and the beam flickered back into weak life. He increased his pace up the tunnel's grade. He didn't need the light. The squelches of his boots produced dampened echoes that guided him up the center of the tunnel. That and the pulse of the blobs, on all sides. Their sentient hatred hummed all around him. Their hatred made his hackles stand on end. They hated him because he wasn't one of them, because they knew they would suffer their torment well past the death of the Sun, past the cooling and fracturing of the Earth, their damnation persisting even as the chunk of rock encasing the cave hurtled through space, their agony fueling the machine's arcane tasks.

He squinted into the unbroken darkness ahead. Should've seen their lights by *now, now, now*. He clamped a hand over his lips. He couldn't tell if his assessment reverberated off the goop coating the tunnel or off the insides of his skull.

An involuntary shudder rumbled through his head. *No no no!* They wouldn't have come all this way just to give up now. *The American would.* Kirk stepped up his pace. If that asshole got his way, then he would rob Kirk of everything. Everything. *Everything*.

A twinkle in the distant darkness deflated Kirk's anxiety. The burn in his calves and thighs amplified as he accelerated. His panting roughened into wheezes, which corrupted into strep-like coughs. His stride slowed to a stagger. But the twinkle grew into a beacon. *Not a mirage.* He lowered his head and trudged up the tunnel.

Kirk raised his eyes. The ambient glow of the American's flashlight suffused upwards and shadowed the creases of the American's puggish features, blackening his lips and eyes down to grim slashes. He straddled the center of the tunnel, as if he too sensed the slow sludge of the damned between his boots. He aimed his flashlight's beam at Kirk's face.

Kirk raised a hand to shield his eyes. He stamped to a stop. His giant swallow scraped along his throat. He struggled to master his breathing. His wheezing reached a jagged apex, then subsided. As soon as he could speak, he said, "I know ... I know where they're going." He summoned the image of the object into the forefront of his mind. The image had seemed sharper back in the chamber. He shook his head. Didn't matter. He knew the object would activate another strange ancient machine. That machine would bring on total annihilation. "We still have a chance to stop it. We still have a chance! I still have a chance, a chance, chance!"

Kirk bared his teeth. He mashed his lips against each other. The American betrayed no indication that he had blurted anything weird. Kirk exhaled, the last dregs of his exhalation bearing the lowest of whispers, "I still have a chance."

He stepped over the trap, intuiting that crossing from this direction wouldn't activate the essence-rendering mechanism. "I was afraid you'd left."

The American raised his other hand. He pointed a gun at Kirk and said, "Stop right there."

Kirk halted. He lifted both hands over his head. The American's flashlight blinded him.

"Not another inch until you explain yourself," the American said.

A cough gathered in the pit of Kirk's stomach, raged through his lungs, and drew a clutter of hacks in its wake that forced Kirk to double over. In the aftermath, he wiped his mouth with the back of his hand. Bloody trails streaked from his knuckles to his wrist. He took shallow breaths until the wheezing subsided. He rasped, "Damn." He straightened and met the American's glare. "You know I went down there to find out where they went." Kirk studied the American. The man wanted to go home. He'd sent the others back so there wouldn't be any witnesses. He could claim anything he wanted, and they would believe him. "Where are the others?"

"I had to send them back."

Kirk nodded. Icy tendrils slithered out from the pulsing mass in his guts. "So you were planning this all along."

The American scoffed. "Planning? I sent them back over an hour ago. I was about to leave myself."

"What?" Kirk rotated sideways. He glanced back the way he came. Fifteen minutes. *Tops*. From the corners of his eyes he regarded the American.

The American's gun did not waver as he said, "You've been down there for hours."

Kirk shook his head. "No." He furrowed his brow. He replayed the American's insane claim and listened for the lie. He sagged. His heightened perceptions notwithstanding, he couldn't catch the tell. Maybe if he knew the American better. But he didn't, and those specific subtleties eluded him.

"The others thought you might have walked into another trap," The American said.

Kirk clicked his teeth together three times. He'd accumulated enough familiarity to detect the treacherous note in the American's tone. The American had hoped that he'd joined the interminable oozing of the sentient, gelatinous blobs. The American's density had to prevent him from plumbing the true depths of the damnation throbbing all around them, but *fuck him* anyways. Kirk shut his mouth. A low growl quivered his clamped lips. He dredged up the bizarreness of the American's claim in order to relax his jaw and neck muscles. Outside, outdoors, even blindfolded he knew he'd perceive the difference in the time of day, pinpointing the Earth's rotation relative to the Sun, but inside the Devouring Cave, inside this infernal machine, time did not exist, nor would it ever. His shivers synched with the sluggish rhythm of the goop.

"I think it's down there," the American said.

Kirk listened to the decay of the vibrations of the American's accusation until the suckling of the ooze swallowed the peaks of the last sine waves. The man's indictment sounded legit to Kirk.

"I think it only sent you back up here to lead us off the trail," the American said.

Kirk's shake of his head grew in violence until he jerked it to a stop. "That doesn't even make any sense … why would I lead you here and then try to lead you away?" He straightened to his full height.

"That's what took so long," The American said. "That's why you were down there for hours. Reprogramming takes time."

Kirk opened his mouth but reined in his protest, emitting only the barest hint of a grunt. *Don't be stupid.* The American didn't need to waste energy by playing a dumb game with him. He only needed to send the others away in order to get away with murder. Kirk had no choice but to entertain the very real probability that this machine, or the mummy itself …

He raked a hand through his greasy hair. He found no point of reference, no purchase, to account for such a discrepancy in time. But given everything he'd experienced since the mummy stirred from his hibernation, he couldn't discount that he might've spent hours down there and not noticed. Considering all the information that had bombarded him, it actually made sense … "It seemed like a few minutes to me … it's possible that it could be down there … but why would it even allow me to lead you this close?"

Kirk placed his palm over the mass in his stomach. It seemed bigger and harder. He did the calculations. *The mummy* stood to gain from such a delay. Because the mummy sensed they were closing the distance, which mattered because … "Oh my god …" and now, because of the delay, they may not be able to catch up, *catch up*, "catch up … it thinks we *could* stop it!"

He refocused on the American. "You see now, right?" Kirk searched for the dawning realization on the American's puggish face. The man might kill him, either now, to bring on the apocalypse, or after they'd stopped it, but he must see now that they had enough of a chance to scare the mummy itself. "Do what you're gonna do, but do it now. She, we don't have a second to spare." He stared at the American's trigger finger. The slightest twitch and he would rush him, and let the chips fall where they may.

"That's exactly what you'd say," the American said, "if the mummy was down there."

Kirk suppressed another bout of coughs, which shook his chest and blurred his vision with tears.

"But I can think of a way to see for myself, " the American said. He lunged at Kirk and jabbed the gun's barrel into Kirk's solar plexus. Kirk slid a half-step backwards. He flailed his arms for balance, casting his flashlight against the tunnel wall. He went up on his tiptoes while grabbing the American's gun arm with both hands. He teetered on the edge of the trap. The blobs squealed out of their stupor, as if salivating for another unfortunate soul to share their torment.

Kirk loosened his grip, thinking to go for the American's eyes, but an eruption of coughs wracked his torso. Blood drizzled from his nose and pattered onto his collarbone and chest. He stole enough breath to shout, "If it was down there I wouldn't be falling apart!"

The American's stare bored into Kirk's eyes. He used Kirk's two-handed grip on his forearm to whip him away from the trap and up the tunnel. Kirk released his hold and stamped in the sticky goop. The American said, "Then I guess we'd better get our asses in gear."

Kirk got his feet centered underneath himself. He wiped the blood from his nose. He wondered if it was too late for him, if proximity could even cure him in the first place, and then, if Lesley was faring any better. He launched himself into a near jog, as fast as his tired muscles could combat the tunnel's upward slope and the gummy footing. The American's squelches matched his own. They still had a chance.

Chapter Twenty-one

Lesley grimaced. She concentrated on breathing through her nose, but the aftertaste of rust had already built up in the back of her mouth. She guessed the rhythmic rattling, of metal wheels rolling over the imprecise linkages of rails, jolted particulates free from the corroded walls of the boxcar. She coughed. The pain of the hack threaded from the back of her throat to the pit of her stomach. She figured the hours of train travel had brought on a case of motion sickness. She tightened the thin, groaty blanket around herself. The growing cold strengthened her impression that they had succeeded in gaining an illegal entrance into Eastern Europe via the Pacific Rim. Still, she knew they were moving in the right direction, satisfying his wishes.

She reached out her right hand and plucked a leaf from his 'throne.' Like the rest of the foliage festooning his raised seat, the leaf remained firm and a lush green. A dense weave of pliable branches, the sapwood glistening at severed nodes, formed a high-backed chair that supported his dormant weight. The sylvan theme extended to the raiment they'd decked him in, including a flower garland, a robe of vines and blossoms, and a gnarled branch as a scepter that she supposed was made of oak. One of the lunatics had declared, 'We sit on the ground, Bacchus sits on high.' She had managed not to laugh in their earnest and crazy faces. She didn't need nor did she want to know any more about their twisted beliefs. So long as they stayed on course.

She balled up the wet leaf and dropped it on the dusty wooden floor. She drew her knees up to her chest. She wrapped her arms across her upper shins. She stared at the faded green of her ratty blanket. Her vision fuzzed. Only total devotion could overcome such ridiculous trappings, and such ridiculous beliefs. The fact that so many shared this total devotion – true believers not so fortunate as to share space with their idol crammed other boxcars on this train – astounded her. She flinched. If the same delusion could infect so many people, then …

She slipped her crossed arms over her kneecaps and pressed them against her chest. If only she could've understood … *anything,* back in the chamber. Her fingers retracted from her biceps and coiled into fists. The promise of revelations composed the perfect carrot to manipulate her. She raised her left fist to her lips. She had witnessed him puppeteering enough people, both in physical and mental terms. All he needed to do in her case was to impart the illusion of self-determination. She mashed the knuckles of her fist against her clenched teeth. He'd driven others to murder. She just didn't know, she didn't know, didn't know … she couldn't dredge up anything tangible to latch onto, nothing exempting her, only blankness behind the memory of her nails tearing into the loose flesh of his stubbly throat, and the splintering of the slender bones in his gullet … she was a murderer.

Pain throbbed from her lips. She dropped her fist from her mouth into her lap. She was *not* a murderer. But if that was true, then he'd made her do it, and so he could've been pulling her strings all along. A rush of hacking coughs rocked her entire body.

After her lungs calmed, she wiped her face with her palms. Her glance raked the others in the boxcar. Slitted eyes schemed out from under dreadlocks and the hems of hoods. Tangled beards hid sneers. Thin blankets betrayed the shivers of the bundled-up forms of the zealots. None of them exhibited the least trace of psychic protection, all of them offered themselves, yearning to be elevated to his 'special.' If he selected one, she knew the rest would at best toss her off the moving train, and at worst rend her to shreds.

She straightened her legs against the gritty wooden floor, stretching her hamstrings. She relaxed her fists. If he wanted a mindless puppet, he could've picked any of these fanatics, for starters. But he'd chosen her. All along the way, he could've gotten rid of her. His choices had run the spectrum. But he hadn't got rid of her. The object held the key to her understanding. She was meant to understand. Perhaps she alone could understand.

A surge of energy swept away her broodings and made her scalp tingle. She looked up as the mummy rose from his throne and shucked his ceremonial twigs and leaves. She jumped to her feet too fast. Dizziness flooded her field of vision. Strong, bandaged hands cupped her shoulders and steadied her. A sense of serenity flowed through their rejuvenated connection. Her mind stabilized. She found her balance.

The cult's raucous reaction dissolved her warm swaddling of peace, growing in volume until their howls and shrieks bunched her neck muscles. They slam-danced against each other and against the rusty walls of the boxcar. She shuffled closer to the mummy, so that her shoulder and hip grazed his bandages. Some whirler's elbow clipped her in the ribs. She pivoted, revolving her back to the mummy. She squared herself to the mayhem, raising her hands and nudging away riotous dancers who spun too close. They stomped their heels, they leapt into the air, they crashed into one another, they hooted and yodeled, and the total avoidance of anything approaching a traditional step emerged as their sole rule.

She shifted her weight back onto her heels. *No rules*. This bizarre cult wanted something approaching anarchy, albeit under their 'god.' They wanted to drag civilization down into shambles. She couldn't see how so many people could share such a warped view. They had no conception of what the mummy intended.

The mummy's bandaged palm warmed her shoulder. Her rigid posture slackened an iota. His palm applied gentle and firm pressure on her shoulder blade, guiding her to a position a half-step behind him at his side. Stillness and silence flash-froze the cult. The mummy raised the oaken branch. The cult erupted. But instead of resuming their Bacchanal, they fell to the crates and footlockers. They armed themselves. Most stabbed assault rifles into the air, but some brandished swords, long knives, or spears.

A gargantuan man, his orange brush-cut seeming to scrape the boxcar's ceiling, advanced towards Lesley and, an assault rifle lying across his upturned hands, proffered the gleaming black weapon to her. The gun's oily odor penetrated the rusty buildup in her sinuses. Despite the cold, the giant had bared his vast pale pectoral muscles and his deep-cut abdominal ridges. Madness sparkled in his green eyes. A Gallic twang infused his words as he said, "We near our destination. Fight beside us, or we leave you behind."

Lesley grabbed the rifle. She reared up to her full height. She aimed her chin at the ginger giant and said, "I go where he goes."

He smirked. "For now."

She glared at him. She knew they wouldn't dare raise a hand against her, but that didn't stop them from hoping and praying that she'd be killed in the coming battle. Zealots every bit as unhinged as these freaks guarded the object. She said, "They know we're coming. They'll be ready."

"Of course," he said. "They must have their own special. But since Bacchus awoke, they must have sent the lion's share of their soldiers into the field. They will not return in time. He chose precisely the correct opportunity to attack."

The floor bucked. Lesley's stomach compressed from the bottom up. Everything tilted. A jarring crash catapulted her headfirst into a mass of bodies. A bony blow to her forehead flickered her eyesight to black. She processed a skidding sensation before a jolting stop.

Lesley squirmed out from underneath limp torsos and limbs. She rolled onto her back and tried to blink away the cobwebs. A weird ticking irritated her eardrums. She shuddered. She rubbed her ears but couldn't get rid of the irksome noise. She feared a concussion, maybe permanent brain damage, then the staccato bursts clarified into gunfire.

A thin rectangle of light on the roof widened as the boxcar's door squealed on its coasters. Armed cult members scaled the capsized car and clambered out into the steely gray, joining the fight. Lesley lurched to her feet. She swayed, then the vibrant current from the mummy sobered her. She located him at a corner of the car. She stumbled to him. He stooped and jammed his hand into a fissure in the car's rusty wall. The damaged metal screamed as he tore the flap upwards, creating a ragged hole in the wall. He stepped through the hole. Lesley snatched up a machete and followed him into the icy chill.

Chapter Twenty-two

The Middle-Easterner wrenched the handlebars. The snowmobile's sudden veer surprised Kirk. He tightened his grip on the Middle-Easterner's waist. They hurtled along the train wreck so fast that Kirk only caught a glimpse of the cardboard drum that the Middle-Easterner had dodged before the far-flung piece of cargo vanished into the unbroken white. Kirk wished they would slow down. The thick snowfall reduced visibility to a couple of sleds ahead of them. They brought up the rear of the peloton, the American, leading, set the breakneck pace. Kirk squeezed his knees against the sides of the snowmobile's seat. If he fell off, even the Middle-Easterner might leave him behind to freeze to death in the storm.

The snowmobile helmet's tinted visor combined with the dense torrent of flakes to soften the edges of the wreck. The rusted undercarriages of overturned boxcars flashed into Kirk's line of sight. He spotted twisted and torn railing. His helmet muffled the roar of their fleet, and also tamped down the stink of burning fuel. His puffy coat and insulated snow-pants kept him toasty for a while, but the rattling hours on the back of the snowmobile had allowed the chill to seep into his gloves and boots. A tingling sensation, the harbinger of frostbite, intensified in his toes and fingertips.

Inside his skull, his psychic link to the mummy spiked to a clear volume, then dipped back into a staticky overlap, that reminded Kirk of those points where two or more radio stations vied for supremacy at the same frequency, and moving the dial a hair one way or the other made one of the stations blare. Kirk suspected that the mummy was well aware of their approach, and it was trying to block the link, or at least warp the signal enough to disguise its source off to the north of the railroad tracks.

A lump in the white snagged his attention. The cocoon of snow stopped at the head of a lifeless man. A circlet banded his long brown locks away from his slack face. A set of … they zipped by before Kirk could squint, but the impression of bull horns, jutting upward from the corners of the dead man's forehead, persisted. Two more snow-blanketed corpses came into view. A bloody man writhing in a dark patch of snow incinerated the stirrings of Kirk's curiosity. Among the immobile lumps, the dying reached towards the peloton.

Kirk's mouth dried. Light coughs bubbled up and echoed within his helmet. He braced himself. The mummy's efforts at distorting their psychic link left Kirk in the dark concerning Lesley's fate. His coughs deepened and roughened. He intuited that he could alleviate his various pains if he just pointed the peloton in the right direction. But he had to know. She might be among the dead, she might be among the injured and dying. She might need him.

He cocked his head. The buzz of the lead snowmobiles had changed course. The American must have found tracks that the storm had not yet obliterated. They wouldn't require Kirk's guidance any more. Despite the mummy's attempts at disruption, Kirk sensed that the mummy's position hadn't changed for some time.

Kirk tapped the Middle-Easterner on the shoulder. Kirk performed a twisting gesture with his wrist, as if holding an imaginary key. The Middle-Easterner eased off the throttle and brought the sled to a coasting stop. He kept the engine running.

Kirk dismounted. His hips, neck, and gut ached from the bone-rattling ride. As the rest of the snowmobiles gained a lead, a weak call for help, from the derailed train, reached Kirk's ears.

The Middle-Easterner shouted through his black-visored red helmet, "I can not guarantee that I shall survive. They may not return for you."

Kirk's nod devolved into a shrug. He pointed toward the north, the swirling snowstorm already swallowing any sight of the snowmobile fleet. "Do you know where they're going?"

"My best guess? A decommissioned missile silo. There were many, many believers in the Soviet Kremlin. Certainly a faction could have transferred such a site off the books, if it ever was on the books. A faction awaiting orders to launch a nuclear missile. Good luck."

The Middle-Easterner revved the sled's engine and swerved around after the rest of them. Kirk waved his arms over his head. He hollered, "Hey!" The Middle-Easterner showed no sign of noticing, then the snowmobile and rider disappeared in the white flurries. Kirk supposed it wasn't important to explain that the mummy wasn't planning to start a nuclear war. He supposed that all of them would rather believe something like that, a mundane interpretation of total annihilation, instead of the snatches he'd gleaned … the static in his brain squealed and forced him to wince. Everytime he strained to see the mummy's endgame …

The squeal dissolved into a series of wracking coughs. He bent over and endured the fugue. The psychic link descended into its familiar background hum. He turned toward the capsized boxcars. He felt the residue radiating from the center car. The car that had carried the mummy. He flipped up his helmet's visor.

He glanced at frost-shrouded corpses as he waded through the deepening snow. Pink and red splashes mottled the white, then dirt and rust nearer to the boxcar. His instincts led him to circle to the short side of the boxcar, where its coupling had torn free from the adjacent car. He slitted his eyes against the flakes whisking through the face hole in his helmet. He zeroed in on the torn flap of rusty metal that created a passage into the car. His helmet seemed heavier. The left side of his neck labored to keep his head level. The mass in his stomach throbbed. He squeezed his numbing fingers into fists. If she was dead, she'd be inside.

He peered into the jagged hole. The car's freight door, now facing the sky, gaped wide open and whiteout light flowed into the car, spotlighting the cascades of flakes onto the pile of snow beneath the door. He ducked inside. He waited for his eyes to adjust to the shadows surrounding the white glow. The metal wall, now the floor, gave a little under his boots. He tromped from body to body, looking only close enough to confirm that each corpse was not her. His breathing went hoarse, a warning that another hacking attack loomed. He picked his way through the debris back towards the hole. He steeled himself for inevitable clutching hand, or roll of wet eyeballs, or weak groan for help. He couldn't help a wounded survivor. He knew he didn't have the guts to put some poor wretch out of his misery.

The unfiltered white blinded him as he stumbled outside. He flipped his visor down and bent over. He squeezed his eyes shut and flipped up the visor. Each cough inflamed the pain in his gut. While hunched over, he plowed through the snow to the next boxcar. He planted his hand against the metal and stabilized himself. Contractions seized his stomach. Dry heaves prevented all but the shallowest of breaths. Dizziness drove him down to his hands and knees, which punched into the drift and caused snow to shovel inside his opened visor. He tilted forward and shook most of the snow out of the helmet. He slapped his palms against the boxcar and levered himself upright. He let the rest of the helmet-invading snow trickle down to his collar. He wheezed, the cold searing his throat, but he managed to get enough air to clear away the headrush.

From the corner of his eye he detected motion. He doddered around and leaned his back against the boxcar. A man, flat on his back in red-stained snow, lifted his head and said, "Hey."

Kirk lurched toward the man, whose arm folded across his chest, and whose hand tried to tie a strip of blood-drenched cloth around the ragged stump where his other arm should've been. Kirk stopped and averted his eyes. The man moaned. Heat sizzled into Kirk's cheeks. He plunged through the snow to the man's side.

Frost streaked the man's eyebrows and blond hair. His face paled to a shade that almost matched the snow. He said, "I'm dying."

Kirk swallowed the lump in his throat. He forced himself to maintain eye contact. The bloody mess darkened the edges of Kirk's field of vision. He rasped, "There was a woman."

"She went with Bacchus."

Kirk tamped down his relief. But the heat in his cheeks redoubled.

The man gurgled, then he seemed to loosen. His fingers ceased their struggle to tie the sad tourniquet. His feeble exhalation produced a gauzy white puff. The man stilled. The color in his eyes faded.

Kirk's spine jerked ramrod straight. The psychic link surged. He missed the first bolts of information, but before the surge died, he gathered enough data to understand that the mummy had known about the booby-trap. It had warned no one, however, not even Lesley.

Kirk sagged. He hissed out a breath. Behind him, the wreckage, the death, was a snapshot of what the mummy intended. He rose to his feet. He plodded into the snow, which was already filling in the snowmobile tracks. He flipped his visor down. The closed helmet muffled the wind, the visor's tint reduced visibility, but his trapped breath warmed his skin. The psychic link swelled and shrunk in sync with the throbbing pain spreading out from the mass in his guts. He tried to ignore the link. He couldn't trust anything the mummy broadcasted.

A faint burst of gunfire corrected his course. The flurries outpaced his plunging gait and filled in the snowmobile tracks. He saw nothing but the flakes swirling out of the whiteness, which towered unbroken maybe ten yards in front of him. At this rate he wouldn't reach his goal until nightfall, he, a loser musician-slash-janitor, against three different sects of crazyass motherfuckers armed to the teeth, not to mention a reanimated mummy dating back beyond prehistory.

He shook his head. That was more of the mummy sneaking things into his brain, trying to dismay him. Nobody else gave a damn about Lesley. He had to keep going. He shredded the psychic assault and discovered a kernel of truth, that the only reason the mummy kept Lesley around was as an insurance policy against him. His link was an accident, a product of the mummy's haste in its escape from the museum. If not for Kirk's acting as a bloodhound …

A harsh cough ambushed him and drove him to his knees. A few drops of blood trickled out of his nostril. The mass cramped his stomach, which instigated a sharp spasm in the left side of his neck. He cried out. He bit his tongue. The mummy, the goddamned mummy did this to him. Couldn't undermine his spirit, so he stepped up his physical agony. A wave of despair kept him on his knees. If that was true, then proximity would not alleviate his physical suffering.

He growled his way to his feet. He leaned into his next step. *More tricks.* His lips parted. The mummy wouldn't bother unless he was a threat to its plans. And despite the mummy's attempts to seed disinformation in his thoughts, he knew the effort cost the mummy great amounts of energy.

Kirk grunted into a quicker pace. He sought other truths in the undercurrent of the link. A cure existed, he felt it in his marrow. He accelerated. If a few minutes of contact with the mummy had left him in such an afflicted state, he could only imagine how bad things had gotten for Lesley. A deep cough raked blood to his lips. The spasms in his neck sharpened. He lowered his stance into the center of his gravity and bulldozed through the snow.

He passed slight bulges in the snowscape, the drifts burying bodies. If anybody had survived the bullets, the cold surely finished them off. He reached the snowmobiles. Just beyond, the snow mounded in a great circle. *No building.* He'd expected, pictured, something like a grain silo. He tracked the pinkish snow, which guided him to a scattering of dead men. He picked up a discarded assault rifle. He worked its strap over his head and slung the gun over his shoulder.

He followed the carnage to an open hatchway, its round, thick iron cover yawning wide on its hinge-arm. He stared down into the hole. An iron ladder, bolted to the circular wall, descended into shadows. He felt the mummy, somewhere far below.

He backed down into the hole. Once all his weight was on the rungs, the ladder vibrated. He wondered how many bolts had shaken free of their housings. A spurt of automatic gunfire echoed to his ears from its source somewhere near the bottom of the silo.

The circular tube ended, and the absence of the wall near to his backside made him tighten his grip and double-check his footing on each new rung. His eyes adjusted to the dim emergency lighting. A glance over his shoulder became a gawk at the tip of a massive missile. His foot eased down onto a wide metal shelf. He lowered his entire weight onto the shelf. He reached out and grabbed the shelf's railing. He imagined the American's reaction, the narrow-minded asshole believing the mummy meant to launch this Cold-War relic.

He eased along the railing, the shelf more of a half-catwalk which took him to another ladder. A few rungs down the missile widened out to its body, curving so close to him that he reached out and touched its shell. As he descended, sporadic gunfire echoed through the silo.

Tremors shook the ladder. He froze. These new vibrations originated from the ladder's bottom, too far down to see. The chaotic patterns implied at least three men, rushing, possibly fleeing. He felt for the rung above. An oscillation penetrated his thick glove. Somebody sneaking down from the topside. He pictured small bands of soldiers trying to outflank each other.

He discerned a ledge a dozen rungs below his position. He hoped the shaking above masked his hurried descent. He stepped off the ladder and hugged the wall. His heels extended over the ledge. His heft stressed the thin iron, causing a slight dip. He found handholds, sharp metal outcroppings, thick plastic cable housings, and he pulled some of his weight off the ledge. He inched around the missile, which gapped just far enough away so that a slip all but guaranteed a plummet to his death.

An iron wheel jutted out from the wall. He spun the wheel and an interior latch clicked. He pulled the hatch door open, its rusty squeal making him cringe. He stepped over the threshold. He closed the door, spun the wheel, but he couldn't find a locking mechanism.

Overhead fixtures, the first few burnt out, shed a yellowish illumination through the low-ceilinged passageway. On his right, a rectangular duct, starting at his ankle and rising to his hip, ran along the wall until it curved out of sight. On his left, thick insulation wrapped ducts that snaked perpendicular into the wall every fifteen yards or so, leaving a gap before another U-shaped set extended into the passageway. Rows and columns of thin metal arms stabbed out from the upper walls on each side.

He stepped onto the torn brown plastic sheeting that protected the iron floor. He lightened his footfalls as much as he could, but he still produced a faint clank with each step. He reached an elevator shaft. He peered through the iron grating. From far below, a loud clang signaled the shutting of the elevator car's door. One of the steel cables spooled upwards, the other downwards.

He ducked and rushed down the passageway. He spotted another wheel on the floor, in a semi-circular nook. The wheel resisted his effort to turn it, then gave a screech while loosening. He pulled the hatch door open. A ladder sank into a cramped room. He knew if he closed the hatch behind himself, pitch blackness would swallow him. Also, the room looked like a dead end.

Gunfire erupted nearby. He shimmied into the hatch and closed the door behind himself. He hung onto the rungs and strained to hear. He lowered himself down to the floor. He bumped into a swivel chair. He caught its back, arresting its grating squeak. He stood still until his heartbeat fell to a distant pulse. He unslung the assault rifle. He realized that he didn't even know if the gun was loaded. He leaned it against the wall. He sat down in the swivel chair. He breathed. He needed a plan.

He laid his hands on the desktop before him. Through his thick gloves, he felt knobs and switches. He removed his gloves. He let his fingers walk over the control board. He snorted. For all he knew, one wrong flick of a switch could touch off a nuclear holocaust. He shook his head. That sort of control room had to be a helluva lot more difficult to get into.

He fondled some toggles. *What the hell*. He flicked one at random. A monitor on a bank of screens fuzzed to life. The picture showed nothing but static, but provided a black-and-white glow that revealed the labels for the switches, buttons, and dials. He bowed his head. All the words and letters featured that backwardsy Russian alphabet. He flicked all the toggles in that particular set. Most of the ancient monitors hummed to life. Some showed nothing but empty corridors. Others showed skulking gunmen. The one furthest to his left forced a groan out of him. The monitor's grainy definition transformed the mummy into a movie monster from the fifties. Despite the blanket wrapped around her up to her chin, despite her attempts to shield herself behind the mummy, he'd recognize Lesley anywhere.

He twitched. His link to her through the mummy crackled to life. Her terror, that the cult guarding the object would detonate the nuclear bomb before allowing the mummy to seize the artifact, blasted into his brain. He had no idea how to contact Lesley, but he tried anyways. She showed no signs of sensing him on the monitor. A weird string of curses shot through the link. He frowned. Not her. Somebody Russian, the cult's shaman or priest or whatever. The only reason they all hadn't gone up in a mushroom cloud was because the man was scared to death.

Kirk stood up. If he knew this, then the mummy knew it too. But the mummy either hid its fear, or was not afraid at all. And if it wasn't afraid of a nuclear bomb …

He grabbed the assault rifle and hurried up the ladder.

Chapter Twenty-three

Lesley pressed her shoulder into the concrete wall. She gained maybe a foot of extra view around the curve in the tunnel. She slid forward, her boot swishing through the ankle-deep water. The low ceiling and narrow walls seemed to close in, and she couldn't help imagining how fast a gush of water might fill this glorified tube. From behind, the mummy copied her creeping gait. She removed her right hand from the machinegun's trigger and wiped the sweat from her brow. Despite the cold, she couldn't stop sweating.

She re-gripped the trigger. Everybody else had died getting them this far. She had to take him the rest of the way. She felt the object nearby. She felt its guardian, the shaman, or whatever, of the occupants of the missile silo. But she had no idea how many gunmen stood in between.

Her next step brought the end of the passage into sight. An iron wheel jutted from the center of the metal door. The mummy's mental exertion caused her to sway as he bent the full force of his will against the shaman, who cowered on the other side of the door. Lesley picked up the man's fear. He'd thought his devices protected him from the mummy's psychic invasions, but all his measures only delayed the inevitable. The shaman's fear resolved into the fear of death. The man teetered on detonating the missile's warhead. Only his doubts about the true nature of the mummy and his terror of death gave him pause. From her vantage in the psychic connection, she sensed that the mummy was stoking these doubts and fears, even as he sought physical control over the semi-shielded shaman.

The metal wheel on the door cranked a notch to the left. And another notch. Then another. One more and the latch clanked. The door creaked inward. A man reeled out of the darkness and over the threshold. A thin black skullcap encased the man's head down to his eyebrows and earlobes. She understood that the skullcap housed the technology that had failed the man. A bushy beard hid all of the man's face except his stricken, bloodshot eyes. The man shook. She didn't understand his rambling mumble, but his tone sounded like begging to her. He held a thin metal disc in one trembling hand. *The object*.

The shaman flicked the object at them. Instinct forced Lesley to dodge the projectile. The shaman ducked back into the doorway. She counterpoised the assault rifle against its shoulder strap with her trigger hand, and fished the object out of the water with the other. She fingered the mismatched notches on one section of the disc's edge. Otherwise, she found nothing remarkable about the thin metal. She experienced no instant insight, not even a wisp of a revelation. She coughed. Nothing. Nothing, *nothing*.

Her hand robotted toward the mummy and placed the disc in his bandaged palm. Her feet skittered toward the doorway. She flailed for balance as the warning that the shaman was completing the last steps in the detonation sequence sizzled through her mind.

The shaman ignored her entrance. He leaned over a massive control board. Wires, with duct-taped connections, snaked over the archaic switches and dials. She gleaned that the shaman was not a hundred percent certain that his jury-rigging would override the board's failsafes.

His fingers clawed toward a doctored switch. She understood that the mummy was slowing the shaman's final twitches, but the shaman was winning the psychic battle a millimeter at a time. The shaman had finally accepted that he would not survive the mummy, and so his last reservations concerning nuclear annihilation had evaporated.

Her feet felt as heavy as lead. She howled. If the shaman threw the switch, then she would lose everything. The object, the object, the object activated a machine that would make everything clear to her. Clear, just like the shaman's attempt to control her through the psychic feedback became clear to her. The shaman preyed on her doubts, feeding her fears that the mummy meant to abandon her now that he had what he wanted, that the mummy had been manipulating her all along ... no, *no*, "No!"

Lesley gunned the shaman down.

She slumped against a giant, antique reel-to-reel computer. She sobbed. She sucked in a shuddery breath. She raised her head. Her wild attack had destroyed several monitors. One intact monitor showed, in black and white, a squadron of armed men stalking through a passage. She assumed the gunmen were closing in. She detected motion out of the corner of her eye.

The mummy swayed to the control board. He flipped a switch.

Chapter Twenty-four

Kirk's coughing fit dredged him out of unconsciousness. He mumbled, "What?" One of his knees lodged against his forehead. Some hard, pointed object jabbed into his left shoulder blade. He uncoiled, finding himself wedged under the desk. He reached out for support and grasped one of the legs of the overturned chair. Pain pulsated from the back of his skull. He groped a hand back there, winced when he brushed the goose egg, but his fingertips came back dry.

Black and white static from a pair of working monitors lit his way to his feet. Pieces of the assault rifle lied among the scattered manuals, the small units of Cold War-era equipment, and shattered plastic. He judged himself lucky that the rifle hadn't gone off and peppered him with slugs. The nanosecond he turned to considering what happened, Lesley's 'no-no-no' reverberated inside his brain. *The warhead*. The mummy was moving away from the silo, *fast*. The mummy and Lesley, rocketing on snowmobiles. He leaned down until his forehead rested against cool plastic. He closed his eyes. Sleep geysered up and threatened to snatch him away.

He wrenched upright. He breathed, "Get moving." He stumbled to his gloves, which had ended up on the floor. He stooped and grabbed them. He stood too fast. A swell of dizziness staggered him back to the console. He got his feet underneath himself. He had to get moving before the mummy escaped for good. "Pull it together."

He put on his gloves. He gripped the ladder and shook it. It felt wobbly. He pulled himself up and the ladder shifted, but it held his weight. He turned the wheel on the hatch door and shoved it. He crawled out into the dim yellow light.

He coughed. The lump in his guts throbbed in time with the goose egg on the back of his skull. He swayed. His knees loosened. He moaned. He tilted into the wall. He felt his way along the dented passageway. He edged through the artificial narrows, the thin metal arms protruding from both walls grazing him at the worst points.

He detected an undertone to his pulsing pains. From Lesley, he discerned, almost inaudible in the psychic link. He concentrated on those blips. Her cough was slight, but persistent. He found an intact ladder rising up into a tube. As he climbed, he tamped down his own urge to cough. He focused on his own stomach, and found her echoes under his pain, but she ignored her own discomfort, chalking it up to lack of food, lack of sleep, and her physical and mental sufferings. He arrived at another hatchway. He spun the door's wheel and clambered onto a catwalk.

Smoke, suffusing the air, forced another bout of coughs out of him. He sidled along the catwalk. Through the haze, the buckled tip of the missile canted far below his position. The corner of his mouth twitched. His brow wrinkled as he diverted his attention inward. He sought traces of that compulsion for repetition, and of that confusion over whether or not the repetition had been spoken or thought. He believed he detected the faintest oscillations, and he also believed that much of their faintness was due to the fact that she was unaware of her compulsion. He could only conclude that her proximity to the mummy masked how sick she really was.

He arrived at a stable ladder. He climbed. The rungs' heat penetrated his gloves. With each upward step, the fatigue in his thighs, his shoulders, and his low back intensified. The sensation of them speeding away from him clawed at his will. He coughed. *Useless.* Even if, by some miracle, he caught up to them … he imagined border guards, Russians maybe, maybe Chinese, demanding that he show his nonexistent papers, accusing him of being a spy, and throwing in some hellish jail where he would finally succumb to the poison sunk deep into his bones and soul. The mummy, on the other hand, would use its psychic powers to pass the border unmolested.

He paused. He leaned out on the rung as far as his arm would allow. Fuck the world. Fuck the world. Fuck the world. Tendrils of smoke curled around him. With his left hand, he let go of the rung. He yawed out over the drop and swung back and forth in a diminishing arc.

A descending glissando, just the barest tickle of the ivories, the lightest graze on the string, brought a dry smirk to his face. "Motherfucker." He chomped his teeth together three times. The whole goddamned time, while he probed for insights into Lesley's condition, the mummy had been fiddling with his own mind, tiring him, slowing him, very nearly coaxing him into a suicidal plunge.

He swung his hand back to the rungs. The smoke cleared as he ascended, and a shaft of gray light cut a diagonal into the silo. The growing cold braced him and brushed away some of his cobwebs. For a moment, as a tiny burst of energy lifted his spirits, he entertained the possibility that all his symptoms were just mental manipulations of the mummy. But he coughed, his stomach hurt like hell, and so did his head and neck, for that matter, and he smelled the blood in his nose. *Wishful thinking.* He was gonna die, soon.

The hatchway lid stood about three-quarters open. A blast of wind chilled him when he popped out his head. He cinched his hood. The snowfall swirled and pelted, reducing visibility to almost zero. The gusts threatened to knock him off his feet. He slanted his body against the wind and tromped through the thigh-high drifts towards where his memory claimed the snowmobiles were parked.

"Figures you survived."

Kirk froze. He squinted into the white flurry, but he didn't need to see the American. He recognized that gruff cadence. Over the squalling wind, the crunches of their footfalls brought four shapes into view. They trained their guns on him. Snow and frost crusted their hats and hoods.

Kirk waved the back of his hand at them. "We've all got radiation poisoning by now, so you might as well drop the guns."

"It didn't detonate the bomb," the American said. "It launched the missile."

Kirk took a second to process this information. He tightened his hood. "But the top was shut, so it … imploded."

"Something like that," the American said. "Killed almost everybody, clearing the way for it to escape."

"With the object." Kirk scowled. The mummy had it, had hid that fact from him somehow, and now the mummy was hurtling toward its endgame. "I can feel it. We gotta get going."

"No."

Kirk coughed. He rubbed his forehead. The pain from the goose egg on the back of his head circulated feelers to the front of his skull. He understood that the American preferred a survivable apocalypse. The kink in Kirk's neck flared. He hissed, his exhalation visible. Kirk understood that the American was worn down too, the man's resolve withered to a nub. Kirk scrambled for an argument, for a tack he hadn't tried on the man, but his own fatigue made his thoughts sluggish. He was so damned tired of trying to convince the asshole that the apocalypse he wanted so goddamned bad was not gonna be anything like he thought it would be. He couldn't see how he could make the man comprehend total annihilation.

One of the others, his facemask muffling his voice, said to the American, "You can go home if you want, but I'm not gonna let their sacrifices go to waste." The other two stood behind the speaker. Kirk realized that the Middle-Easterner must be dead. He scanned himself for a reaction, but he was too burnt out to mourn for his kindest kidnapper.

The American swiveled and faced his comrades. Kirk couldn't help noticing that the man seemed to pantomime gunning the others down, the way his assault rifle's barrel swept from one end of the trio to the other. "Fine," he said. "To the bitter end, then." He pointed his left hand into the blizzard. He said to Kirk, "Lead the way."

Chapter Twenty-five

Fat raindrops pelted the station wagon's windshield. The tired sweeps of the wipers created just enough visibility for Lesley to see the road. The darkness, the hum of the tires, and the wipers' hypnotic sways coaxed a yawn from deep in her guts, a yawn that threatened to unhinge her jaw. She could hardly believe that soon she would be home. She wouldn't have believed it while the wind whistled through the holes in the twin-engine plane that carried them over the sea. At the Alaskan airstrip, they'd 'borrowed' the silent and robotic pilot's station wagon. She wouldn't have believed that they would make two successful border crossings on the back roads to Oregon. The mental effort of manipulating the pilot, as well as the border officials, seemed to have sapped the mummy. The constant driving had sapped her. She could hardly believe that in only a matter of minutes after a stop at the museum, she would be asleep in her own bed.

She took the familiar exit off the interstate. The exit curved right into the museum's neighborhood. The dark rain-slick street relieved some of the tension in her neck. *Home.* She eased off the gas pedal, dropping from highway to city-street speed.

She glanced at the mummy, who hadn't moved in miles, not so much as a twitch since they crossed the border that last time. The puffy coat's hood shadowed his bandaged face. His coat, snow pants, and boots hid the rest of his wrapped body, as well as the strange, perforated disc. She guessed he might have twitched underneath all that material. But their psychic connection maintained the lowest of hums. She expected something more, some indication of excitement now that they were almost in sight of their goal.

She hit green lights all the way to the parkway. She cruised right into the parking space in front of the museum. The brick three-story façade brought tears to her eyes. She shifted the station wagon into Park and killed the motor.

The rain strafed the station wagon. Water cascaded down the windows. The damp cold penetrated her own coat. A cough rumbled up from her lungs. She knew she was sick, her temperature up, she'd probably be bedridden for a few days. She only had to muster enough energy to get him back into the museum. She didn't have anything extra in the tank to worry about what would come afterwards. She didn't think she could haul him inside. She'd get a dolly. She nodded. She groaned. Hunger gnawed at her belly. She shouldered the door open and used the door's frame to drag herself to her feet.

The passenger door scraped open. She pivoted against the car and slumped until her forehead grazed the station wagon's wet roof. She allowed herself a moment of trembles before she mastered herself.

Behind her, other doors opened. She wheeled. Across the narrow street, the side door of a parked van slid open and revealed gunmen.

Lesley backed up against the station wagon.

From the sedan's back seat, Kirk stared through the rain-blurred windshield. The American had chosen to stake out the museum from a position a block north and on the parkway parallel to the narrow street in front of the museum's back entrance. The drizzle, the darkness, the distance, and the park's trees and statuary thwarted their sight line. Kirk had zero chance of identifying the passengers of the station wagon. But he understood the American's reluctance to occupy a closer space. Any of the vehicles parked up and down the streets could contain armed nutjobs, who hoped and prayed that their 'god' would return.

Kirk hoped and prayed for someone else. He tuned into that psychic channel. A high-pitched squeal made him flinch. He fingered the electronic buds crammed into his ears, even though his short experience with the jamming devices had taught him that adjustments did nothing to soothe these irritating spikes.

He coughed. He sniffled up a trickle of blood. The mass in his guts throbbed in time with the pain in his neck. Ow ow ow! He glanced at the American, who sat in front of him, then he looked at the driver, then he side-eyed the pair sharing the back seat with him. Nobody gave any indication that he might've spoken out loud.

He pressed his fist against his lips in order to stifle the next round of coughs. He'd lost track of her before the American insisted that that he plug the jamming buds into his ears. He'd lost track back before they boarded the private jet staffed by a trio of seething men who reminded Kirk of the Middle-Easterner. He knew she'd been suffering the same symptoms. Exposure to the mummy might've killed her already. He gnawed on his knuckles.

An amorphous figure exited the driver's side of the station wagon. Kirk leaned toward the windshield. The person slumped over the station wagon's hood. *Yes!* Despite his horrible vantage, despite her bulky coat, he'd know her body language anywhere.

He bowed his head. The mummy must've been striving to keep him from homing in on them. Blocking an awareness of Lesley must've been a ploy to dishearten him. The mummy, after crossing the ocean, had turned south. It didn't take a genius, or a psychic link, to realize where the mummy was going. He guessed the American wasn't absolutely sure that this was the mummy's final destination, or the asshole would've abandoned him long ago.

The others murmured. Kirk raised his head. The mummy lurched out of the station wagon's passenger door. A buzz penetrated the earbud's defenses. He choked back a cough. The equipment was not a hundred percent effective. The mummy might be able to possess the others.

Across from the station wagon, a squad of dark-clad men leapt out from a van. Kirk's spine snapped straight. His left hand found the door's handle. The buzz inside his skull flared into a roar. He gritted his teeth. He detected motion at the top of a church's steps. The homeless person popped up from his cardboard bedding and threw away his sodden blanket. Kirk spotted more, scrambling up from the doorways of the buildings up and down the block. He grabbed the American's shoulder. He said, "Look."

The American swiveled his head back and forth. "Shock troops."

Kirk pointed at the highrises and apartment buildings cramming the blocks. "It could raise an army if it had to." He opened his door. "Follow me. I have an idea."

A man stumbled between Lesley and the lead gunman. The rain had plastered his sparse hair to his skull. Water dribbled out of his long, tangled beard. One end of a sodden blanket, wrapped around his calf, clung to him while the other muddied end trailed behind him.

The gunman hesitated. The man lunged at him and wrenched backwards. He tore the assault rifle out of the gunman's hands. His back whapped against the street. His arms flopped behind his head. The assault rifle skittered underneath a parked car.

A woman limped out from between the van. She threw her squat bulk into another gunman. A soaking man circled around the front end of the van and attacked. More followed. They came fast, so fast they seemed to glide over the ground, as if invisible strings swept them into the gunmen. They wrested guns from their victims. They discarded the weapons instead of using them. Lesley nodded. The mummy meant to keep the battle as quiet as possible, in order to delay the inevitable arrival of the police.

Lesley spun and hurried to the museum's back entrance. The mummy's footsteps plodded behind her. She punched in the security code and unlocked the door. She held the door open for him. The door closed and hushed the grunts and snarls of the battle outside. The interior's warmth washed over her. She locked the door and rushed after the mummy.

One of the American's men forced the gate's lock. Kirk exhaled. He wouldn't have enjoyed climbing the fence, he doubted he even could scale the tall black metal bars, which curved outward in order to keep the homeless from squatting in the cement stairwell that led down to the church's basement door.

Kirk followed them down and through the lower door. He guessed if the first break-in hadn't set off the alarm, this one would. He calculated that they had five minutes at the most before security personnel, or the cops, responded. He snorted. The mummy's instigated brawl in the street would occupy the authorities, at least long enough for the mummy to do what it needed to do.

Déjà vu overwhelmed him as they hurried through the dim church basement towards the adjoining door to the museum. He wondered if the American experienced the same reminder of where he first captured Kirk. He'd bet anything that if the American could go back …

The lead man seemed to not even slow down as he barreled through the splintery door. Kirk shook off his reveries. He suspected the mummy was still trying to manipulate him, trying to divert his attention from the task at hand. Kirk ran into the shadowy museum basement to find the others waiting for him. Waiting, waiting, waiting for him to point them to the machine, so they could destroy it, and then he could explain to her that the mummy had been lying to her all along, and if he could just open her eyes to the truth, maybe she wouldn't hate him. Fuck, fuck, fuck! The mummy was doing it to him again!

The American swept a hand towards the stacks of boxes and the big wooden crates. "Where is it?"

Kirk resisted the temptation to scan the contents of the dusty basement. He had no fucking clue, but he couldn't tell the American that. He also had no fucking clue how the machine would bring on total annihilation. They needed the mummy to tip them off. But he'd bet anything that the sarcophagus was the machine. "Upstairs, the exhibition." At worst, they would meet the mummy coming down the stairs. But first, he needed to take a precaution. He hustled to the elevator, and exhaled relief to see the car already on the basement level. He raised the rickety wooden gate an inch. The gap would prevent the elevator from engaging, forcing the mummy to take the stairwell, if the machine lied somewhere among the bric-a-brac in the basement.

He dashed to the stairwell. "Follow me."

Lesley skidded to a stop behind the mummy. Clomps resounded from the basement stairwell. They weren't even trying to be quiet. More misguided zealots, must've been lurking in the dark, just in case. The mummy saw no use in veering either way along the intersecting hall. This last group would interfere, maybe spoil everything, waste every sacrifice. She coughed, she sniffled. Whatever he did to them, they would be the last necessary victims.

Their heads manifested in the dark landing. Their wet nylon jackets caught enough of the dim radiance to glisten. Deep, grating hacks exploded out of one of them. Lesley frowned. *Kirk?*

Lesley's neck whiplashed as her body careened toward Kirk. She screamed. One of his fellows shoulder-tackled her in the guts. She folded in half over him as she let out a big 'whooof.' She had a split second to anticipate the impact of her skull against the tiles, and then the image of a cracking egg filled her mind. Their tangled limbs and torsos whirled ninety degrees in mid air. Their sides slammed onto the floor. Her hands, of their own accord, clamped to the sides of his head. Her fingers clawed the electronic plugs from his ears. Her body rolled away from him. She flopped onto her back. She groaned. Her nerves tingled. She flexed her fists. She was back in control.

Gunshots deafened her. The man she had attacked laid on his back, but held his head up off the floor and both his hands gripped a handgun, which he fired at the landing.

A high-pitched squeal assaulted Kirk's inner ears and drove him to his knees. A distant scream penetrated the sonic onslaught. The others jostled him. A gunshot caused the others to scatter. A thigh smashed into the side of his head and the impact knocked him sideways down the stairs.

He pawed at the risers. He slowed the descent of his upper body, but his legs kept going until he straightened over the stairs. He dug his toes into a riser and stopped his tumble. In his right ear, the squealing decayed, but in his left ear … the left side of his head jerked upward, as if a giant invisible fish hook had stabbed into his eardrum and yanked him. He winced. He noted the gunshots, but he couldn't stop his left hand and foot from crawling up the stairs, the right half of his body stroke-limp.

He dug his right-hand fingers into a rubber stair-tread. He braced his right boot against his left-side's slow attempt at an ascent. He realized his fall had dislodged his left earbud. He resisted the upward tug, which strained, then snapped, and his full weight collapsed across the steps. The mummy had bigger fish to fry.

The faint lighting darkened. He raised his head. The American, just a silhouette, but his posture giving away his identity, loomed on the landing above, pointing a gun at Kirk. The American said, "Get up."

Lesley followed the mummy into an anteroom off the main gallery in the wing housing the Rewrapped Mummy exhibit. She had packed the cramped room with exhibitions that bore loose relations to mummy culture, hoping to pique the interest of wandering patrons. Now the room seemed so … *busy*. She'd selected every piece, and even she couldn't process the glut of artifacts.

The mummy seized a simple bronze helmet from a display. She recalled including the hoplite gear on account of a correlation between Egyptian and Greek culture. She understood, in a flash, that the mummy had taken great pains both to obscure the true value of the seemingly unremarkable headpiece, and to contrive that the museum would acquire and store the piece until his arrival.

She narrowed her eyes. Before her suspicions took shape, the mummy discharged a burst of instructions. Among the helmet's embossed decorations, a number of knobs protruded. One of the disc's notches fitted a specific knob. Once locked in, the disc would spin, not in a perfect circle, but off center, sort of like a gyroscope.

Nothing too difficult. She searched her memory for how they had procured the helmet. She found nothing. The museum must have acquired the piece before she took over the reins. The mummy must have been orchestrating this 'coincidence' for years. The helmet, the museum near the Pacific Coast, even leaving the helmet behind lest they lose or damage it during their quest for the disc.

The mummy sat. He pressed his spine against a display case. He groped around the back of his skull. He peeled away a strip of bandage. Small puffs of dust spouted up from the dry undersides of the otherwise damp strips. He discarded the strips in a small pile beside himself. He placed the helmet over his skinless, blackened skull.

Lesley wheezed. Her wheezes harshed into coughs. She inhaled the faint tang of metal polish. Her mind seemed to de-center. She placed her left hand on a display case in order to steady herself. She tasted tin foil. She coughed. A weird snapping sensation, deep in her head, made her reel backwards. She wilted down to one knee. She leaned her shoulder against the display case. A range of aches and pains pinged from all over her body. The painful compression of her kneecap against the hard tiles gained dominance over the other injuries. Rain pelted the outer wall. From the other side, footsteps, like explosions, sounded from the hallway. All the nearby objects appeared to tower over her. She blinked. Everything receded, settling back into their proper proportions.

The mummy tucked his chin against his chest, exposing the back of the helmet. Lesley's fingers traced the notches and cutouts in the cold metal disc. She felt like she swayed back and forth while being lowered into herself. She felt *reduced*. She felt like she flailed for her end of the psychic connection, but she couldn't find him, couldn't get a grip on him. She didn't remember feeling this way before …

Her brow furrowed. She tried to remember how far back her depression over the world at large went. Way before the advent of the mummy, certainly. But when had it sharpened, and heightened, that was the question. She cast her scrutiny back to the day-to-day worries of her undergrad education, then to the extreme immersion of her grad-school struggle, six grinding years to that doctorate degree. The sheer mass of minutiae created an impenetrable fog. She just didn't know. But certainly the chance to make a difference had lifted her out of her gray despair.

A tiny whine escaped her lips. What else? This machine had to make everything clear. A way to synchronize and parse his thoughts so that she could understand them. She found no reason why the mummy would have gone to such lengths to deceive her. If all he needed was a stooge, he could've swapped her out at any time. An unquestioning zealot would have served nefarious purposes much better. The only possible reason he would preserve her through everything was that she was necessary too. He would've lurked in her thoughts, influencing her, only because this whole thing, this whole undertaking, was so fundamentally fantastic that she would not have accepted it otherwise.

She nodded. She pushed herself up and stepped towards the mummy.

Kirk dropped to his knees. The American dragged him back up to his feet. The American kept his gun's barrel against Kirk's kidneys. Kirk knew it was useless to explain that the psychic link had died. The American had forced him to shuck the other earbud. The American was using him as a shield, as bait, as a diversion, so that when the mummy tried to possess him, the American would make his move. And if the American had to kill him in the process … he imagined the American shrugging.

They entered the small room. The American shoved Kirk into a display case and opened fire. Lesley's scream clipped short. Kirk thrust himself to his feet. He didn't see Lesley. The American emptied his gun into the mummy, riddling his torso with holes. Plumes of dust puffed up from the black punctures. The mummy removed its strange helmet, revealing a decayed skull. The psychic link hummed back into the middle of Kirk's brain.

Lesley sprang out of an aisle and tackled the American. They sprawled away from the mummy. Kirk gritted his teeth and strained with all his might, but he couldn't move. They wrestled. Kirk felt the mummy's influence surging through Lesley, bestowing enough extra strength to grapple the American to something like a draw. But sooner or later, he would overpower her.

Kirk managed to scuff his right foot forward. The mummy sent him a promise, the gift of musical genius. Kirk flinched. The mummy sent him an image of the disc, lying in the aisle, and then the simple instructions of how to fit the disc onto the machine, the helmet.

Kirk scoffed. Even if the mummy was telling the truth, even if the mummy possessed the power to grant such a gift, and it wasn't just another trick, what good would musical genius be after total annihilation?

Chuckles, growing to dry laughter, reverberated through the psychic channel. The mummy corrected Kirk's notion of total annihilation. The mummy pulled up Kirk's memories of the sentient sludge in the Devouring Cave.

Kirk shook his head. He mouthed, 'No.' If that was true, then musical genius was next to worthless.

The mummy sent another image, a sequence of images, the American killing Lesley while Kirk stood still as a statue, unable to intervene. The mummy assured Kirk that once the helmet was back on its head, both Kirk and Lesley would be released. If Kirk didn't comply, the mummy would remove the helmet, allow the American to murder both Lesley and Kirk, and then the mummy would try to convince the American to satisfy its wishes.

The mummy replaced the helmet on its rotted head. Kirk felt the channel die. He hurried to the disc.

A coughing attack forced Lesley onto her side. She flopped onto her back. A metallic click drew her eyes to the gunman, who stood, one palm flat against the butt of his gun. *Reloading.*

Lesley's stomach cramped. She doubled up, lifting her torso and legs off the marble tiles. Her vision tunneled, telescoped, the gunman seemed to skim far away, shrinking. The gunman raised his weapon, and he whooshed back into magnitude. The see-sawing perception dizzied her.

The gunman fired. Lesley pivoted on her ass. Her dizziness grew. She lurched onto her hands and knees. She crawled into the gunman's shins and knees. Her lack of force dismayed her. He planted his boot's sole against her shoulder and drove her backwards. She tumbled onto her ribs.

A whirring penetrated her hazy perceptions. The whirring distorted into an irritating grind. She shuddered. The grind halted to a sudden silence. Lesley battled her descent into unconsciousness. She pawed at the base of a display case and pulled her torso upright. She crawled around the display case. Droplets of blood dripped from her nose and pattered on the tiles.

She stopped. She blinked. Kirk lied in the aisle, a pool of blood spreading out beneath him. Bullet holes mottled his chest and face. He didn't move. She slapped her palm into a blob of stickiness. The goo pulsed. She tore her hand free, the substance adhering to her hand before ripping loose. Her disgust propelled her sideways, and her elbow struck the helmet. The disc spun a half rotation. Sodden bandages, empty, outlined the absent figure of the mummy, from the neck down. She rifled through the bandages. *Nothing, nothing, nothing*!

She whirled around and slammed her back against a display case. Her motion jostled the helmet. She coughed, and with each cough, she felt … smaller, and smaller, and smaller.

She grabbed the helmet and jammed it onto her head. She groped for the disc, and she spun it. Flashlight beams raked her. Hands grabbed her and threw her onto her belly. They seized her fists and pinned them behind her back. Cold steel clasped around her wrists. She shrieked, No, no, *no*!

www.ingramcontent.com/pod-product-compliance
Lightning Source LLC
Chambersburg PA
CBHW060618130626
46555CB00002B/560